I0749363

ENTWINED

IRON BULLS MC #3

PHOENYX SLAUGHTER

Entwined (Iron Bulls MC #3)

Digital ISBN: 978-1-943950-91-1
Print ISBN: 978-1-943950-83-6

Edited by PREMA
Cover Designed by: AJ Lake

ENTWINED

(IRON BULLS MC #3)

In Entwined, the highly anticipated third book in the Iron Bulls MC series, shocking secrets and desires are revealed. Can Dante and Karina's passionate bond survive or will they be torn apart?

CHAPTER ONE

KARINA

BEING in the same clubhouse where I've had some raunchy and sometimes public sex usually turns me on. Not today.

After the president of the Iron Bulls MC so casually informed me that my father has another family, we all went back to the clubhouse to "chat." So now I'm seated at a table—not the official table where the club has church—with my boyfriend, Dante, Romeo, and my father. Uncomfortable doesn't adequately describe this scenario.

Dante's been making murderous faces at my father since before the bombshell announcement. He hates my father for many different reasons.

My father nods at Dante. "Karina, how did you two meet?"

Before I open my mouth to answer, Dante places his hand on my knee and leans forward. "Better question is what the fuck kind of father leaves his daughter alone to fend for herself for so long, you piece of shit."

My father's shrug of indifference hurts so much, I have to avert my eyes. "She's smart and capable. I've never had to worry about her." It may sound like a compliment. But to me it just sounds like a convenient excuse.

Dante shakes his head. He sits back, but keeps his hand on my leg.

Romeo's gotten tired of being ignored. "The real question, Tucker, is how you plannin' to work off your debt? Because from what I hear, Kadence is tight with the Savage Dragon's VP."

A pained look crosses my father's face and he glances at me with tired eyes. "She doesn't need to be here for this."

Romeo sits forward, placing his elbows on the table. "Oh, I think she does." He focuses his gaze on Dante. "I'm sorry, brother. Until you told me you thought she was his kid, I had no idea."

Dante remains silent, but the tension radiating from him has a life of its own.

Romeo's scary eyes move to me next. "Your father's got a pretty serious gambling problem, sweetheart. About three years ago I bailed him out of trouble. Since he was never going to make enough to pay me back in cash, he offered a trade."

"You fuckin' shittin me?" Dante explodes, throwing his fist onto the table with enough force it rattles the thick oak. He seems to have grasped what Romeo's explaining right away, while I'm still in the dark. Whether Dante's pissed at my father or Romeo, I can't be sure.

"Relax, brother. I ain't gonna touch your girl. Ol' Tucker here's just gonna have to come up with some cash now."

My mind's spinning from everything Romeo just laid out. I can't deal with the fact that my father apparently tried to sell me off for a gambling debt. My own father treating me as if I'm some disposable whore? That's too disgusting to contemplate. No. Instead, my mind latches onto one thing and one thing only.

"Who the hell is *Kadence*?"

Dante

Killing Karina's father right in front of her is probably a bad idea. But it's a battle not to wrap my hands around his fuckin' throat and throttle the life out of him.

"I want to be clear on what you're tellin' me, prez. My girl's father offered, what exactly, if you took care of his debt?"

Romeo sits back, a sadistic smile curling his mouth. He flicks his gaze at Tucker. "He offered me one of his virgin daughters."

Next to me Karina lets out a harsh sob and my vision swims red.

Tucker's real quick to defend his worthless ass. "It's not like they're making it sound, Karina. I figured I'd introduce you, and you'd get along." He glances at me and shrugs.

What a piece of shit.

"Who's Kadence?" Karina asks again. Her voice comes out clear and strong even though her body's trembling.

"She's your half-sister," Tucker finally answers.

"I don't understand. How? Mom—"

Romeo—like the jackass he is—watches the family drama with a smirk that I want to punch right off his face. Him taking joy in my girl's misery is pissing me the fuck off.

"I had an affair with your mother. Met her when she

was waitressing at one of the truck stops. She had you and I moved her down here, so I could still see the two of you."

"Hence the gambling. What with two families to support and all," Romeo chimes in.

Ignoring Romeo, Karina sits forward. "But Mom died years ago. Why didn't—"

"I couldn't tell my wife about you. She would have used —it doesn't matter now. We divorced shortly after your mom passed away."

"Then why were you still gone all the time?"

Fucker's got no answer for his daughter.

Like I said, he's a worthless piece of shit.

"Did you tell Logan to stay away from me?"

Tucker opens his mouth—and by the seedy smile on his face he's planning to lie through his teeth. "Don't fuckin' lie to her," I growl at him and he snaps his mouth shut.

"Yes," he finally answers.

"Why?" Karina lets out a miserable sniffle. "He actually took care of me when you were gone all the time."

Tucker flaps his hands in the air. Christ, his daughter has more spine than he does. "I was fixing to set you up with Romeo and I couldn't have Logan fuck that up."

Romeo snickers like an asshole.

Karina sniffles. When Romeo sees the tears rolling down her cheeks he stops laughing.

"He broke my heart because of you?" she asks. The innocence in her voice fuckin' shreds me.

"I'm sorry, Karina. I didn't have a choice."

"The hell you didn't!" she snaps at him and I'm proud of my girl. "You're the one who sent that guy to *talk* to me, aren't you?" She swipes the tears from her cheeks and stares her father down, waiting for an answer.

Tucker's guilty gaze swings away and I lose my fuckin' shit. "You set your own daughter up to be molested? What the fuck's wrong with you?"

Both Romeo and Tucker explode out of their chairs. Next to me, Karina whimpers and grips my hand tighter.

Tucker stutters and shakes his head. "What are you talkin' about? I never—"

"You hire men to deliver a message like that to a beautiful teenage girl all alone. What the fuck you think was gonna happen to her?" I ask, dropping each word low enough for Tucker to sense he's skating close to getting a bullet in his empty head.

He spreads his hands out in a helpless gesture. This fucker isn't nearly as concerned as he should be about what he's put his daughter through. "Karina, I just couldn't have you keep sniffing after Logan. He was only supposed to scare you. Not hurt you. I'm so sorry." The apology seems to come as an afterthought and the urge to kick him to death makes my feet twitch.

Ignoring her father, Karina turns to me. "Dante, please, can we go now? I've heard enough."

I raise an eyebrow at Romeo who nods.

I stand and she follows. Her father doesn't say a thing.

If Romeo doesn't put this waste of air in the ground, I swear to fuck I will.

CHAPTER TWO

KARINA

As soon as we're out in the main room, away from the insanity of my father's betrayal, Dante pulls me into his arms. There's a good chance Romeo might kill my father and I can't call up an ounce of concern. That probably makes me an awful daughter, but I honestly don't care. All I feel when I think about my parents is a lot of *nothing*.

"You okay, baby girl?"

"No. I'm not okay at all."

His mouth tightens into an angry line. The need to get away from the clubhouse claws at me. "Can you take me for a ride?"

"Yeah. Anywhere in particular you wanna go?"

"No. As long as I'm with you, it doesn't matter."

Once I'm tucked onto the back of Dante's bike my head clears and everything I learned today sinks in.

I have a sister.

I was the product of an affair.

This explains my father's long absences.

No wonder my mother drank.

He takes us to the first restaurant we ever ate at together and I smile at the memory. On our way inside, he takes my hand calming me and making me feel safe at the same time. We sit in the back and there's no one else around us. The place is quiet at this hour.

"Feeling any better?" he asks after the waitress leaves.

"I feel better being with you. But about my family? No."

One of his big, warm hands slides over mine. "Baby, I'm your family now. The club's your family. You don't have to waste another second on that guy pretending to be your father."

"Thank you." More of the afternoon sinks in. "Dante, would Romeo have really taken me to pay off a debt? I don't understand."

His face hardens and he squeezes my hands a little tighter. "I don't know what the hell their arrangement was all about, baby girl."

"And my sister? I can't believe I have a sister. I wish I'd stayed to find out more about her."

"I'll help you find out whatever you want to know. Promise you that."

His words make my heart jump. "Thank you. It's weird. I always wanted a brother or sister. And I've had one this entire time. I wonder if she's older or younger?"

"Probably older."

"Do you think she looks like me?"

"Don't know. No clue what her mama looks like. Doubt anyone's as pretty as you though."

He always knows what to say to make me feel better.

"Can we go home, Dante?"

"Yeah, baby girl. Whatever you want."

I'm so...torn. I don't know how to express myself or how to process everything.

When we step in the front door, I turn and slump against Dante. His arms band tight around me, strong and comforting. "What does my baby girl need?" he murmurs next to my ear.

"I don't even know."

"Got homework?"

"Shit. Yes. It's in the car, at Romeo's shop."

As if they'd heard me, two cars pull into our driveway. One is my new car. The other I recognize as a truck from Romeo's shop. While Dante goes to meet them, I hang back in the kitchen.

All three men stomping into the house rattle me. Luck's been here before. But Romeo hasn't. And I always feel uneasy or off-balance in his presence.

Dante holds his hand out to me. My signal that it's okay for me to join them I guess.

"Thanks for bringing my car up," I say to Luck, who nods at me. Dante hands over my backpack and I set it by the stairs.

The living room seems to have shrunk in size with three big men taking up so much space. My man is the biggest, but the other two aren't far behind. They're just as scary, too. A skitter of fear brushes over me.

I've been around these guys at the clubhouse plenty of times. But this is more intimate. Strange having them in our personal space. What if they decided to hold me down and do whatever they wanted to me? I'd be powerless to stop it.

A different sensation prickles over my skin. Excitement. A tingling spreads all over as I picture the three of them—

As if he hears my perverted desires, Dante turns my way. "Here're your keys, baby girl." His words draw Luck and Romeo's attention to me again.

My heart hammers and my panties are definitely damper than they were a few minutes ago. Now it's the combined focused attention of all three of them making me squirm.

"You okay, baby girl?"

I'm still standing there like an idiot instead of taking the keys he's holding out. "Yeah. Um, tired." I grab the keys and set them on the counter. "I'll leave you guys alone. I've got homework." Romeo smirks at the word "homework." My face burns with shame.

I turn and take the stairs two at a time before I do anything else to embarrass myself.

Dante

"What's up with her?" Romeo asks after Karina races upstairs.

"You really have to ask after that fucked up situation with her Dad?"

For once Romeo shows some compassion for someone other than his dick. "Yeah. That was fucked. Think she's worried I'm—"

"Don't even finish that thought."

"I ain't gonna touch your girl." He almost seems offended.

"Go check on her," Luck says.

Romeo nods and the idea of my prez telling me to take care of my woman over discussing club business makes for a massive what-the-fuck moment. What a day.

Karina emerges from the bathroom just as I'm about to call out her name.

"Oh." She slaps her hand over her chest. "You startled me. Did the guys leave?"

"No. Wanted to check on you." My gaze lingers on her face. Flushed cheeks, wide eyes. Travels lower. Neck and chest also pink. Hard nipples straining against her tank top. "Are you okay?"

Her bottom lip trembles and her cheeks turn even pinker. "Yes. I—" she gestures at her backpack over by the bed.

"Homework, yeah, I know."

I'm still studying her as I crook my finger and motion her closer. "Come here."

When she's standing in front of me, my hands settle on her shoulders giving her no option other than facing me. Except, she keeps her gaze lowered and it's buggin' the fuck outta me. "What's wrong?"

"Nothing."

"Take your clothes off."

Now she meets my eyes. "What? Why?"

Leaning down, so we're almost nose to nose, I lower my voice to explain the situation to her. "Because, baby girl, I don't think you're telling me the truth."

"And taking my clothes off will help?" Ah, there's the bit of sass I like from her.

My fingers trail over her shoulders and down her arms. "Yeah. I know how to get the truth out of you."

"Dante. Luck and Romeo—"

"Will wait downstairs until I'm finished with you."

Her breathing picks up, but she's still rooted to her spot. Still got her clothes on. Tightening my hold on her arms, I turn her around. "Put your hands on the wall."

She hesitates. "Dante—"

"Did I *ask*, baby girl?"

"No."

This time I wait. Staring at her until she's spread out like she's waiting for a police pat-down.

The kind I'm about to give her isn't the lawful kind.

As usual, I'm struck dumb by how fuckin' perfect every inch of her is. I get up real nice and close behind her. Run my fingers over her bare thighs, up under her shorts, then back out. My fingers work the button and zipper open enough for me to squeeze my hand down the front. Nope, still too tight. I yank them down and they bunch up around her feet.

She's completely still. When my hand connects with her ass, she jumps and squeaks. "Step out." She finally gets it and kicks the shorts to the side.

"Hmmm. I like you in white. Gotta get you more of these." My hand's running all over her ass and hips, then dips under the front, sliding down until I hit the jackpot. With my free hand, I brush her hair over one shoulder and kiss right up to her ear. My fingers slide easily through her slit. "Spread your legs."

She slides her feet a few more inches apart. A soft moan passes her parted lips, then a louder one, as my middle finger slides inside her.

"Why so wet, baby girl?"

Her arms tremble and I'm afraid she won't be able to hold herself up much longer. My arm bands around her waist, holding her tight. I slip my finger out, drawing her wetness up, teasing and circling her clit.

A needy whimper comes out of her mouth.

Two of my fingers slide in her tight hole and I take my time pumping them in and out.

"Tell me. And don't lie."

"I can't."

My teeth graze her shoulder. Enough to make her shiver but not mark her. "You can tell me anything."

"I don't want you to be mad."

What the fuck could I ever be mad at her about?

"Oh. Oh. Please," she whines. "Harder."

"Not until you tell me what I want to know."

Christ, I've conducted a lot of interrogations through my years with the club. None of them were ever this much fun.

None of them ever got me so fucking hard.

She sobs and shakes in my grasp. "I was scared downstairs."

That makes me stop. Her hips keep moving seeking relief. "Scared of what, baby girl? Luck and Romeo? They'd never hurt you."

"I know." She hisses as I resume pumping my fingers in and out of her. "I know you'd never let anyone hurt me."

There's something she's holding back. "What else?"

"Please don't make me say it."

Of course now I *really* want to know. "You gotta, baby. You can't keep any secrets from me. Especially if it's something that upsets you."

"I was scared. I thought the three of you could hold me down and do whatever you wanted to me, and I wouldn't be able to stop you," she says in a breathless rush. So fast, I almost don't catch all the words. Her pussy squeezes my fingers and she's so wet, girl juice's dripping down my hand.

"The idea turned you on."

"Yes," she sobs. "I'm sorry."

I mash my lips together so I don't laugh and make her feel bad. My thumb rubs over her clit and she whimpers. "Don't be sorry. You can't help what turns you on. I want you to tell me all your dirty thoughts."

"You're not mad?"

"Fuck no." Christ, she's fuckin' innocent. "Now, if you'd stripped downstairs and yelled out 'Come fuck me' then yeah, I'd be pissed."

She laughs. A soft sound that turns into a moan as I increase the pressure of my thumb.

"I don't think I can share my baby girl with anyone. And I'd never let Romeo touch you. *Ever*. Just so you know."

"Good," she sighs.

"Ready to come now?"

"Yes, please."

Fuck, I love this girl.

"Lean back against me."

She's so eager, I end up chuckling against her ear. My hand circles her wrists, pinning them between her breasts. She's already close. A few quick thrusts in her snug little cunt are all she needs before she's moaning and writhing in my arms.

It takes her a few seconds to open her eyes and when she

does, my heart slams against my chest so hard she can probably hear it. She blinks up at me, her lips curving into a soft smile. "Thank you, daddy."

"Love you, baby girl."

"Love you, too." Her hand reaches down and rubs over my dick. I'm harder than a motherfuckin' hammer and having her hands on me ain't improving the situation.

"Not right now, baby girl." I gotta calm the fuck down. I've probably only been gone less than ten minutes, but I still need to get back downstairs. "Finish your homework. I gotta take care of some things. After they go, I want you ready and waiting for me to fuck you—*hard*."

CHAPTER THREE

DANTE

I TAKE a lot of shit from Romeo when I finally get downstairs. It's possible they heard Karina's moans and shrieks a few minutes ago and I find I don't really give a fuck.

"Christ, you reek of pussy," he bitches.

"Fuck off, you jealous prick."

"Amen to that, you motherfucker. Stop being such a greedy asshole and pass that bitch around."

"Are you fucking high?" I growl at him.

He smirks, but knocks his shit off.

Luck remains silent during our exchange. Finally, he pipes up. "Romeo filled me in a little bit. She handling it okay?"

"What? Learning her father's a useless piece of shit who tried to sell her for a gambling debt? Or that he's a two-timing fuck with another family stashed away and a sister she's never met? Because, no she ain't handling none of that well."

"Sorry, brother."

Pulling a few beers out of the refrigerator, I motion for them to sit at the bar in the kitchen. "Tell me."

Romeo opens his mouth—I think to play dumb, then thinks better of it when he sees my face. "Tucker's always been a fuck-up. Only thing he does well, is run that big rig. Whatever it is about him, he never gets pulled over, searched, ticketed, nothing. He's just got that square look to him, ya know?"

Always looked like a pansy-assed cocksucker to me, but I tend to be a bit cynical.

"Shit started missing from our hauls, envelopes came back light. Turned out he was making detours to gamble. And losing big. Fuckers he was running around with stole one of our shipments."

I vaguely remember when that had happened. Romeo had been real adamant that he be the one to handle it.

"I bailed him out of that fucking mess and as payment he said he'd give me one of his daughters. I thought he was fucking joking at first. Our MC's never been involved in pedaling pussy."

"Then where'd he get that idea from?"

"Who the fuck knows. He probably watches too much television. But if he had 'em pledged to me, I figured he wouldn't be sellin' 'em off to anyone else."

I highly doubt Romeo's intentions were that noble, but I keep that thought to myself for now. "Yeah, and what were you plannin' to do when it was time to collect?"

He waves off my question. "I'm more than capable of finding bitches to spread their legs for me. But the club needed him to keep moving our stuff, so I temporarily let it slide."

"You know the other daughter?"

"I know *of* her. Her mama dumped Tucker's ass and hooked up with Savage Dragon's prez. Tucker almost shit himself. Begged me for protection."

"That how we got into it with them?" Our beef with their MC had been more of an annoyance than anything. It passed with a low body count and our clubs are on okay terms for now.

He shrugs. "They're pricks."

One false move could easily blow our truce to hell. This right here is why doing business with fuck-ups like Tucker bothers me. But I ain't the prez, so it ain't my call. No, my job is to protect the club when Romeo's decisions put it in danger.

"You know about the guy he had come talk to her?" I swear to fuck if he was in on that, prez or not, I'll crack this beer bottle over his head.

"Fuck no." He seems sincere, almost insulted I'd even suggest it. "I didn't take the fucking thing all that serious. Tucker introduced me to Hemi. Never told me he was his daughter's boyfriend or anything of the sort. First time I met your girl was when you brought her in. Even then I didn't know who she was."

"Okay." Fuck me. "You think Hemi knew?"

"Maybe."

Fuck. Him taking her makes a lot more sense if he somehow found out about the debt and thought she was about to be sold off to Romeo. Gonna make it difficult to slit his throat if it turns out he was trying to protect her in his own stupid way. Still plan to beat the daylights out of his disloyal ass when I find him though. Taking her from me. Trying to turn her against me. That can't go unpunished.

"So where we at?" I ask before I work myself into a rage over Hemi.

Romeo eyes me longer than I care for before answering my question. "You planning to claim her soon?"

Luck stares at our president. Fuck, I do, too. That question ain't a good sign.

"I don't know, prez. I was thinking, maybe she ought to graduate from high school before I bend her over the table and fuck her in front of the entire club." I barely manage to conceal the sarcasm from my voice.

"Don't get twisted, Dante. I ain't saying I'm gonna touch your girl. But you know as well as I do, word of that bargain gets out and she's unclaimed...that ain't gonna look right."

Ain't gonna look right for *him*. Makes him look weak. But you don't earn a president patch in an MC like ours because someone hands it to ya, and you sure as fuck don't *keep* it because someone lets you, so I understand his concern.

Still pisses me off.

He strokes his hand over his chest, something he does when he's thinking. "I hear what you're saying about school."

"How much is he into you for?"

"Hundred K."

"That's it?"

Romeo raises a brow. "You wanna pay his debt?"

No, I don't fuckin' want to pay his debt. It will put a serious dent in the money I'm startin' to think of as

Karina's college fund. But I also don't want to rush her into something she ain't ready for.

Since I'm still working this out in my head, Romeo opens his mouth. "Don't stress. I'll keep working on that dumb prick. When's graduation?"

"Two weeks, I think."

A different smirk lights up his face. "Her little friend's got a birthday right after, doesn't she?"

"Yeah," I answer wearily. Christ, from the sound of it, he's got the date circled in red on his "Girls I need to fuck" calendar.

"Maybe you bring her by the clubhouse for me, and I'll wipe this whole thing clean."

"You wanna let a hundred thousand dollar debt go for a taste of her friend?"

He lifts his shoulder, but he's not fooling me one bit. "I'm really not all that worried about it."

Luck turns to me. "I don't think the claiming has to be a big deal. Ease her into it slow."

"Yeah. It's happening eventually anyway. Just thought I'd let her finish school first."

"Two fuckin' weeks," Romeo says.

"No, I mean college."

Romeo pulls a face. "What the hell does a hot little fuck like her need to go to college for? Knock her fuckin' ass up."

And people think I'm a caveman. "She's smart. Thinkin' about med school. Thought the club could use a doctor."

Asshole actually stops to think about it. "She's that smart?"

"Yeah. And the thought of having fuckin' rugrats around withers my dick, anyway."

Romeo laughs like a jackass. “I hear you.” He pretends to check the watch he’s not even wearing. “Well, it’s probably her bed time. We should go so you can get one last fuck in.”

“Those jokes never get old, prez.”

“I’m glad.” He slaps me on the back on his way out.

Luck stops and bumps my fist. “You need anything let me know.” His tone all serious and straight-faced.

“Thanks, brother. Appreciate it.”

Once the place is locked up tight, I shut the lights off and head upstairs. Knowing my babygirl’s waitin’ up there for me gets my dick harder with each step I take.

Karina

I can’t stop quivering after Dante leaves. That’s what he does to me. Leaves me in a puddle of emotions every time we touch. Every time I breathe him in. There’s a small piece of me that wonders if it’s healthy to be so obsessed with this man. This man who’s so much older and more experienced than me. Although his methods were... unique, I’m glad I confided in him about my unsettling fantasy.

Every now and then I catch the guys’ voices from downstairs. Part of me wants to creep into the stairwell and listen in on their conversation. Part of me is terrified of what I might hear. Eventually I lose myself in my school work. Once I’m finished, I notice a missed call from Athena and call her back.

“Where were you?” she demands. She’s so dramatic sometimes.

"Homework. Phone was off, I just saw you called. What's up?"

"Are you alone?"

"Yeah," I answer slowly. "Dante and the guys are downstairs."

"What guys?"

Damn, she's a nosy pain in the butt tonight. "Romeo and Luck."

"I should come visit. Romeo's just...agh, I can't even."

"He's a little old for you."

"Look who's talking."

I walked right into that one.

"Athena, you don't even know anything about him."

"Sure I do. He's hot and he looks at me like I'm the most interesting thing in the room."

"Yeah, because he probably wants to fuck you."

"And your point is?"

"Did you call for a reason?"

Athena's giggles ring through the phone and I realize I haven't spent a lot of time with my best friend lately. I miss her. Even if she is a pain in the ass. She ends up reading me a short story she wrote for English class because she wants my opinion on it. As usual it's brilliant.

My praise is short-lived. In the background, I hear yelling.

"Shit, Karina. I have to go."

She hangs up before I get a chance to say goodbye. Not unusual. Her parents have always been strict about her bedtime. It almost seems like it's gotten worse instead of better.

Dante, homework, Athena. All great distractions to

take my mind off the mess that is my family. Only a few hours away, I have a sister. How many times growing up did I wish I'd had someone else to talk to or share things with? Someone to hide under the bed with when my mother was on one of her drunken rampages? Will my sister hate me when she realizes she has a bastard half-sister? Romeo mentioned she was seeing someone in a motorcycle club too, and the idea makes me laugh. Pulling my laptop back out of my bag, I run a quick search online, but nothing comes up for Kadence Rivers.

How could my father leave me after my mother died to be with his other family, knowing I was all alone? If he truly cared about me, wouldn't he have told his wife about me, no matter the consequences? Once they split up, why did he still barely spend any time at home? The cynical part of me snorts. Maybe he has a third family out there. I could have brothers and sisters all over the country for all I know.

Thinking about all of this, depresses me. Instead, I focus on Dante. On shedding my clothes. Turning the lights down. Throwing a pillow on the floor and kneeling on it while I wait. Wait for the only man who's ever really cared about me.

CHAPTER FOUR

DANTE

The bedroom's only lit with a soft glow from one of the bedside lamps. I strip my shirt off as I step in the room, tossing it in the corner. Only then do I notice my girl.

Naked.

Sound asleep.

On the floor.

Sliding my arms under her body, I lift her. "Why're you on the floor, baby girl?" I whisper. She stirs and loops her arms around my neck.

"Waiting for you," she murmurs.

I set her on the bed and she curls up, eyelids fluttering. Yeah, she's fucking beautiful and fuck do I want to stick my dick in her, but she's so soft, sweet and innocent in sleep, I can't disturb her. Quickly, I shed the rest of my clothes and slide into bed. I'm almost asleep when she rolls over and tucks herself against my side.

"I thought you wanted me?" she whispers. Soft breath brushes over my ribs.

"You were sleeping."

"Mmm."

She's quiet again, but her tits are all mashed up against my side. Hard little nipples poking into me. How the fuck am I supposed to sleep now? My caveman side's at war with the good guy I don't know how to be. Nudging her onto her back, I lean down and take one ripe nipple between my lips and suck and until she gasps, coming fully awake.

Caveman wins.

"Tell me why you were on the floor, baby girl," I rasp out between sucks and nips.

"I...uh...I was waiting for you."

"How? Tell me."

"On my knees," she whispers so low, I barely hear her. I think my dick hears her before my brain does because he's fully awake and ready to fuck after that admission.

"What'd you want?" My hand threads into her hair, pulling back so I can get at her neck. Under me, she squirms, her legs fall open, cradling me so fucking perfect.

"You."

"Yeah, what else? Want me to stick my cock down your throat?"

"Yes." She rolls her hips, lifting and offering herself. My cock twitches, loving every minute of our teasing game. "You on board to fuck, baby girl?"

"Always."

Fuck if that's not the truth. Her legs are already spread wide, but I shove myself more firmly between them and drive my cock home. "Fuck."

She moans and raises her hips. "Need more, baby girl?"

"Yes. Give me everything."

As if there's anything I won't give this girl. In *and* out of bed.

"So good," she moans as I slowly drag my cock out.

Yes, it is. My hips snap into her at a quicker pace, trying to drive myself so fucking deep, she'll feel me tomorrow. Her little hands slide into my hair and she pulls me down for a kiss. Demanding kisses for Karina. It's a hell of a turn on.

I pull back and roll us until she's straddling me. "Ride that cock and make me come, baby girl. Your man's feeling lazy."

She giggles softly and leans back, resting her hands on my thighs, thrusting her breasts in the air. In the darkened room, I can just make out the hard tips of her breasts jutting up and my fingers close over them.

"Move, baby girl." I pinch and roll her nipples until she raises and lowers herself. Once she gets into it, she's unstoppable. Thank fuck, we ain't got neighbors out here, because she screams like a wild, hungry kitten.

"Dante, I'm coming." She gasps and stutters the words. On each down thrust, she grinds into me hard.

"Good girl. Come on that cock. Get my balls nice and wet." She's beyond words. Watching her, feeling that snug heat squeezing the life outta my dick, I explode about two seconds after her.

She's still trembling as she falls down over me and somewhere I find the will to move my arms, wrapping them tight around her. "You okay?" I ask after planting a kiss on her sweaty forehead.

"Mmm-hmmm." She rolls to the side, but stays close. "Thank you." She shifts and moves to get out of bed but my arm clamps around her.

"Where you going?"

"Bathroom."

"I like my cum dripping out of you, baby girl."

She gasps as I rub my finger in small circles over her pussy, then shove one deep inside. "Dante," she whispers, an urgent plea.

"Wanna fuck you again. I like you being my little dirty girl." My thumb brushes over her clit and she jumps. "Tender?"

"Yes."

The scent of her pussy and sex fills the air, working me up even more. The head of my dick's coated in her juices. "Want that freshly used pussy around my cock," I mumble as I spread her wide and push inside her.

"I want. I want."

I pound into her hard. "Yeah, what do you want?" I grunt out.

"Fuck me."

I chuckle against her ear. "Already doing that, baby girl. What else?"

"Hold me," she answers. There's a quiver to her voice as if she's not sure what she wants. Or I'm just slamming her so hard she can't get the words out. It's hard to tell.

My hands twine with hers, and I push them up over her head, pinning her to the bed. She wriggles against me, arches her back, shoving her tits in my face. "You okay?"

"Hold me. Harder."

This is new. But so fucking good, I keep going at her

like an animal. Holding her down while she struggles, fucking her raw. Under me she's soft and small, but fighting like a little wildcat. "You coming for me, baby girl? Need to feel your pussy choke my dick."

"Dante!"

I press her harder into the bed and she goes fucking nuts. Coming, screaming, thrashing, pulling me with her. I pull out and cum coats her pussy, thighs and belly. The intensity of it rocks me so hard, my head's spinning. "Fuck, Karina."

When I realize how hard I'm holding her arms, I let go and she wraps them around my neck, lifting herself to kiss my face. "IloveyouIloveyou," she murmurs over and over. My hands frame her face, holding her still. "You okay?"

She nods frantically, turning to kiss my hand.

"Let's clean you up. You need to get to sleep."

"Okay."

Carefully, I pick her up and carry her into the bathroom. She's quiet while I soap her up and down. Her arms are ringed with red from where I held her down, and I still her to examine the damage. "This may bruise, baby girl. Didn't mean to get carried away."

"I liked it," she whispers.

Huge, scared eyes stare up at me and I can't help rubbing the back of my hand over her cheek. "It's okay."

When we're finally clean, I slip a T-shirt over her head. Less chance of her tits brushing up against me and my dick zeroing in on her snatch like a damn heat-seeking missile.

Karina

It's so warm and snuggly in bed, I don't want to get up the next morning. It takes a second before I realize I'm alone. Disappointment turns my mouth down, but I throw back the covers and hurry through my morning routine. The scent of breakfast pulls me downstairs.

Dante's cooked for me plenty of times. It's still charming to find my big, gruff, crude biker scooping eggs out of the pan and pouring juice into glasses for us.

"Morning," I announce. My breath catches when he glances up. Crap. Beard scruff and mussed hair makes him totally sexy.

"Hey, baby girl," he rasps. "Sleep okay?"

I nod and slide onto the bar stool opposite from him. He eats standing up, watching me carefully. When I'm finished he takes my arm, examining the faint blue marks around my wrist. They're nothing tragic. You can't even tell what it is unless you study my skin.

"Shit," he grumbles.

Slipping my arm out of his grasp, I shake my head. "I'm fine."

"Maybe you need some padded restraints."

My heart thumps at the word restraint. "Maybe," I whisper. My eyes lower to my lap so I can get out my next thought. "That's what I was thinking about last night. You, tying my hands behind my back. Attaching the ropes to the foot of the bed, and..." I can't finish.

Dante places a finger under my chin, lifting my head to meet his eyes. "And?"

"You know."

He smirks at my shy response. "Shoving my cock down your throat and fucking your face?"

Heat streaks through me. How does he do that with a few simple, crude words?

"Yes."

He nods thoughtfully. "You still got your little plaid skirt?"

Peeking up at him through my lashes, a slow smile curves my mouth up. "Yes. Why?"

"Want you to wear it for me again." His words flow over me like silk.

"I can do that."

We stare at each other for a few more seconds, before he flicks his gaze to the clock behind me. "Better get ready for school."

God, that feels so wrong. I end up chuckling as I slide off the stool and stuff a rogue book into my backpack. I feel Dante's heat behind me, and his hands cup my hips, pulling me against him. I straighten up, shifting against his crotch a little just to hear him groan.

"You need to go, before I strip you down and fuck you."

"I might like that."

He spins me to face him. "Yeah, I know you would. But I want you to finish strong this year. Few more weeks, right?"

"Right," I whisper.

"Good. Where you at with your internship and summer classes?"

Surprised he's concerned about that, it takes me a second to answer. "Still waiting to hear back on the internship and I still need to register for the class."

"Okay. Make sure you get it done."

"I will."

Before I walk out the door, he pulls me to him for a blistering kiss. "I should be here when you get home."

I'm too dazed for words, so I end up nodding.

CHAPTER FIVE

KARINA

School's a drag. Everyone just wants to get to finals and get the hell out of here. No one seems to be able to sit still for very long. Including me. Even Athena's more antsy than usual.

"How'd your dad end up taking you and Dante?"

She'd been there to see part of what went down, but not long enough to hear all the gritty details. I'm not sure I'm ready to talk to her about my half-sister. The whole situation is humiliating for many so many reasons.

"I don't think he knew what to do."

She lifts her shoulders. "Not much he *can* do. It's his fault you have daddy issues in the first place."

"I don't have *daddy issues*. What the hell does that even mean?"

Athena makes this *God, you're fucking dense* face that I kind of want to smack.

"Whatever you say, *baby girl*."

"Fuck you."

Her mouth tips up in a wicked smile and she leans in

closer. "I think that's my problem. I need to get my cherry picked."

"I think it's "popped."

"I know. I was putting my own unique spin on it. Don't you pay attention in English?"

Spin. Athena's making my head spin today. She's all over the place.

"Wait, what? What about Bobby?"

"Doesn't count. We didn't get *there*." She taps her finger against her chin. Something she does right before she asks you something she shouldn't.

"Do I really have to wait until after my birthday—"

"Yes."

Her eyebrows do a little dance. "Maybe I'll stop by Romeo's shop and see if he wants to give me a tune-up." She follows that up with a shoulder-shimmy that attracts the attention of the boys at the next table.

I can't help laughing. "God, you're awful. And stay away from him. I don't think he's what you want for your first time."

"Why? He's probably good at it."

"He's gross."

"What are you talking about? He's hot as sin. Besides, I want to screw him, not marry him."

Naturally, she says that loud enough that half the cafeteria hears her.

"Yo, Athena, you need to get fucked, I'll be more than happy to provide a good pounding." Jeremy—one of the most obnoxious guys in our school—shouts.

Athena wiggles her pinky finger in the air. "Sorry, I need something bigger."

I snatch her hand out of the air, holding it against the table. "You're awful. Now they'll never shut up."

Right on cue, a bunch of insults get hurled our way. Jeremy calls *me* a whore, and five seconds later, one of the guys I recognize as a prospect from Dante's club punches Jeremy clean out of his seat. A hush falls over the cafeteria as kids wait to see if a fight will break out. But another kid—who I also recognize—joins the prospect. The two of them are fucking scary. They definitely study at Dante's school of intimidation. The first one leans over and has a brief conversation with Jeremy. Brief because Jeremy gets to his feet and leaves the cafeteria without another word.

The prospect—Cricket, his name finally comes to me—walks by and winks at me, then he and his friend are gone.

"Holy shit. What was that?" Athena whispers.

"He's a prospect at Dante's club."

"Wow. So he's got little minions around watching out for you?"

"No. I don't think so. He probably just recognizes me from being there with Dante."

But it makes me wonder. I can see Dante either asking the kid to keep an eye on me or—"He probably just wants to score points with an officer so he'll get voted in after graduation."

"I'll score with him any day. He's hot. How come I never noticed him before?"

"Because you're too busy lusting after guys who are too old for you?" I offer sweetly.

Athena isn't easily insulted. "True story."

"Hey, I'm thinking of cutting gym and going to the mall before I go home. Do you want to come with?"

Her lips push into what I think of as her *kicked puppy pout*. "I can't. My mom has this stupid interview set up she wants me to go on." *Kicked puppy* turns into *determined bitch* pretty quick with Athena though. "I hate breaking it to her, but I have *zero* intention of sticking around a single day after graduation."

"Are you still thinking of going to California?"

"Hell, yes." She cocks her head and stares at me. "I always thought you'd come with me. There didn't used to be anything holding you here."

I blow out a breath. "Athena. You didn't tell me until a couple weeks ago that you were planning to do that."

"I know. Are you really going to stay here and settle down with him? You're so young. He'll have you spitting out kids in no time."

"No. He wants me to go to school."

Now she looks at me like I'm nuts. "Really? I didn't think those guys were really into their women getting all educated and stuff."

"Stop being a bitch."

"No, I'm serious. Aren't biker wives, like hairdressers and stuff? If they do anything besides look after their man." She says "look after their man" as if it's the most horrible job a woman has to endure.

"There's nothing wrong with being a hairdresser. Why are you suddenly being such a snob? You sound like your mom."

Her face twists. That's probably the meanest insult I could come up with in Athena's mind.

A look of guilt flashes over her face. "You're right. I'm

sorry. I just don't want to see you throw your life away on this guy because you're all sex-fogged-infatuated with him."

I clench my jaw so hard my teeth make this squeaky sound that echoes painfully in my ears. "I'm not throwing my life away. He wants to put me through medical school for fuck's sake."

That finally shuts her up. She sits back in her chair and pins me with an apologetic stare. But I'm too pissed to forgive her right now.

"Are you going to marry this guy?"

"What do you care? Why are you being so nosy today?"

"I'm worried about you. You're young now. What if when you're a thirty-year-old hag he dumps you for another eighteen-year-old?"

I'm done with this entire conversation. I gather my stuff and stand so fast, my chair tips over. "I survived before Dante, and if that happens, I'll survive again."

But inside I'm sick at the thought of a life without him.

Dante

Karina's barely out the door when I get a text from Romeo calling us all in for church. At the moment, I feel like seeing him about as much as I feel like banging my head against the closest rock. Last night's conversation didn't land in my head right. Romeo hinting that I might have the option to buy out Tucker's debt with cash or pussy irritates me. It shouldn't. Shit like that goes down all the time in my world. This time it's too personal. Although I've only met her a couple times, the thought of handing Karina's feisty friend over to Romeo to do hell only knows what kind of perverted shit to, bothers me way more than it should.

Christ, loving Karina's made me grow a conscience. How inconvenient.

Romeo's in a mood when I get to the clubhouse.

"What's wrong, prez?"

"Had a break-in at the garage last night."

That's a bad sign. Everyone in a hundred mile radius knows who owns that shop. "They take anything?"

"No. They tried to open up file cabinets, go through my desk. Shit like that. Don't know if they were lookin' for cash or somethin' else. Either way, there ain't much there."

"Could be kids."

"Gonna make two of the prospects camp out there for a couple nights."

"Good idea."

Before we go in the chapel, Luck pulls me aside. "There may have been a Hemi sighting. Heading toward the East Coast."

"What the fuck would he be doing out there?"

"Don't know. You okay if I bring it up at the table?"

Now this is interesting that Luck came to me with this first. "Yeah, brother. Thanks."

The first item on our agenda is the break-in.

Luck signals Romeo and gets the nod to speak. "Any chance it was Tucker?" He doesn't explain why Tucker might do something so risky, which I appreciate.

"If it was, he's even dumber than I thought."

One patch-holder and two prospects get assigned to stay overnight at Romeo's shop. Poor bastards.

We go over the schedule for the week. Got a protection job Thursday night. I glance at Luck to see if he's up for watching Karina and he nods. Otherwise, I've got a light week, which is fine, because I have a lot of ways I plan to keep my girl occupied.

With that in mind, I take Luck aside after our meeting breaks. "Think you can show me some of that crazy bondage shit you're into?"

He laughs at my assholish question. "Karina interested?"

"Maybe."

Like the nosy bastard he is, Romeo overhears us and opens his big mouth. "Since when are you such a fucking pussy? Tie her ass up if you want to."

Luck stares at our prez with a barely controlled look of disgust, which Romeo is, of course, oblivious to.

"There's not much fun or challenge in that," Luck explains as if he's schooling a kindergartner. "He's twice her size. Overpowering her isn't a question. Having her *trust* him enough to hand herself over and be at his mercy. There's no bigger high than that."

High. Good way to describe the way I feel when I'm fucking Karina. Luck tends to get real poetic about all this shit. All I'm interested in is tying my girl down and fucking the hell out of her in some kinky as fuck positions. But whatever. I've seen the knot work Luck's capable of so if I have to listen to his *submission is a gift* lecture to get some tips, it's worth it.

"I'm teaching a workshop on Japanese-style rope bondage for the Kink Society over in Nobel if you want to come."

"You're teaching a what on what where?" Romeo asks. "People need a class on how to tie a bitch up?"

Talking about this in front of Romeo's giving me an urge to punch something—him.

"Send me the info and I'll see if can make it." Why the hell not?

CHAPTER SIX

KARINA

I'm so pissed, I end up leaving school early. Dante's question about my schoolgirl skirt keeps ping-ponging around in my head. I think that skirt's actually in our room at the clubhouse. No way do I want to stop by there on my own—even though he's told me I can go there whenever I want to and let whoever's at the front door know who I am.

Part of the reason I'm so mad is that I know Athena's questions make sense—even if she voiced them in the most offensive way possible. I *should* be worried about those things. If I'd been given a set of parents who gave a shit about me—like Athena's—I'd be asking myself those questions, too.

How do I explain to her—or to anyone really—what he's done for me? I don't mean material things. More like the intangible stuff I've never had. Safety, security, a happy home to return to after school. All of those thoughts are bubbling through my brain as I wander from store to store gathering things to surprise Dante.

The skirt's hard to find this time of year. I end up

finding one in a store that caters to junior high girls. It's on clearance in the uniform section and the salesgirl gives me a strange look when she realizes I'm buying it for myself and not, oh I don't know, my little sister. She gives me an even dirtier look when I grab a button down blouse, too. No, it's never going to button up over my chest, but then again, I don't need it to.

It's on the tip of my tongue to say something sassy to her, like "Don't worry honey, I'm only wearing it to get fucked in." But I don't.

Next I find thigh-high stockings with frilly bows at the top and a pair of high-heeled Mary Janes. I must already own like three pairs, but these are red patent leather with sky-high heels. The color matches the skirt I bought perfectly.

I've got plenty of hair ties in my car, so that's covered. My last stop is a chocolate shop. Dante's not a big sweets person, but I noticed he does indulge in chocolate peanut butter cups once in a while. Besides my body, I've never given him anything, so I grab those. A cynical voice in my head—probably Athena's—says it's not really a gift since I'm using Dante's money to buy it.

Enclosed in my car, I text Dante to find out where he is. The idea of walking in the front door, all dressed up and surprising him won't leave me alone. He answers right away.

Home, baby girl.

Well, that messes with my plans a little.

I could run back inside the mall and change, but I'm not thrilled about the idea of walking around the parking lot dressed up like a porn-star-hooker.

Instead, I stop at the end of our driveway, shimmy out of my clothes and into my newly purchased sexwear. As I twist my hair into two long braids, I find myself humming along to the radio. Preparing myself for Dante has almost made me forget my fight with Athena and all the doubts it raised.

Once I'm finished, I'm eager to see Dante and hurry up the driveway.

And find *two* motorcycles parked in front of the house, Dante's and someone else's from the club. Romeo or Luck. I'm not sure. The only bike I've committed to memory is Dante's.

Shit.

I glance down at the skirt barely concealing my thighs. My breasts spilling out of my shirt, tied off above my navel.

If it's Luck, it will be embarrassing. If it's Romeo it will be mortifying.

"Karina?" Dante calls from the front porch.

"Be right there!"

Shitshitshit!

Dante ducks back inside before I get out of the car, so he doesn't see what I'm wearing until I step into the house.

Luck's sitting on the couch and both of them turn and stare at me. Well, at least it's Luck and not Romeo.

Slowly Dante crosses his arms over his chest. All his bulging muscles popping and flexing distract me for a minute.

"That's not what you wore to school today," Dante says.

Luck's mouth flattens. I think he's trying to hold in his laughter.

Heat sears my cheeks. I feel like an idiot.

Dante crooks a finger, urging me closer until I'm standing in front of him. "Explain."

My gaze darts to Luck who's watching us carefully.

"This morning...you mentioned, the uh...and I remembered it's at the clubhouse and I wanted to surprise you but I didn't want to go there by myself—" My words come out in a jumbled rush, but he gets the gist.

"I should probably get going," Luck says as he rises from the couch. Dante walks him out and they speak in low tones on the porch for a few seconds while I stare at my shoes feeling like a silly little girl.

The quiet click of the front door pulls my attention off the carpet.

Dante approaches, a small smirk playing over his lips. "What am I gonna do with you, baby girl?"

Dante

Fuck me, but I have to be the luckiest motherfucker on the planet.

Off the cuff, I mention that sexy little school girl getup she has. What does my girl do? Goes all fuckin' out. For me. Just because it will please me.

I'm fuckin' hard thinking about it and she's right in front of me. Tiny plaid skirt, smooth pale skin, tight white shirt tied under her breasts. Breasts that are spilling out for my hungry eyes to feast on.

Without taking my eyes off her, I drop down to the couch and hold out my hand. "Come here, baby girl."

She takes slow steps until she's standing between my

knees. My fingers land on her outer thighs, slowly trailing up under her skirt.

"I'm so embarrassed," she says.

"Why? Because Luck saw you all hot as hell?"

She nibbles at her bottom lip and nods.

"Ain't got nothing to be embarrassed about." I take a second to sweep my gaze over her sexy fucking outfit one more time. "Now, explain how you had time to go shopping and get home this early?"

Her gaze strays to the front door. "I, uh..."

"Yeah?"

"I left school early."

I raise an eyebrow and wait for more information before deciding what to do. Something's wrong with my girl. She won't say any more but I know there's more to her story.

"Karina. I'm waiting."

My hands rise, skimming up and over her ass, squeezing her cheeks. Still nothing.

She stares at my lap, and one of my hands leaves her warm little butt and takes her hand, tugging her down. "Come here."

Yeah, that she's familiar with. She plants her knees on the couch next to me and drapes herself over my lap.

"Why you being a bad girl today?"

"I'm not."

"Mouthy too," I mumble as I flip her skirt up. My fingers hook into her panties, sliding them down but leaving them at her knees. Fuck if I don't have to take a minute to appreciate the sight of her bare ass, waiting for my hand.

The first swat isn't the playful kind I usually give her and she flinches. She turns her head, but I land a smack on her other ass cheek before she gets a word out.

"Ow!" Her feet kick and I almost get a stiletto in my ear. I stop and slip her shoes off, dropping them to the carpet with a muted thud.

"Are you ready to answer?"

"What?" she screeches as my hand spanks her again.

"Why did you leave school early?"

I don't ease up on how hard I'm whacking her ass. "Daddy! It hurts."

"I know, baby girl."

"Athena and I had a fight," she yelps.

My hand stops mid-air. "Sit up."

She sits back and jerks her underwear up, then rubs her hands over her ass. The motion makes her tits pop out of the skimpy blouse she's got on. After a few seconds, she places her hands on her thighs and stares up at me with watery eyes.

"What'd you fight about?"

Her bottom lip pushes out and she glances around the room.

"Karina."

"You," she finally whispers.

"What about me?"

She waves her hand in the air, but I catch it, holding her still.

"I don't know. Stuff like if we were going to get married or what will I do when I'm old and you leave me for another hot eighteen-year-old."

The word, *married* punches me in my gut, knocking the air out of me, so I ignore it.

"Come here." I arrange her so she's straddling me and we're facing each other. Having her hot little pussy in my lap wakes my dick right the fuck up.

I press my palms to either side of her face so she can't look away. "You're the first eighteen-year-old in my life. Fuck, when I was eighteen...never mind. Point is, I ain't with you 'cause of your age. Yeah, I picked you up because you were hot and down-to-fuck, but I didn't move you into my house because of that."

"I know. At least...I think I do."

"Babe, more likely scenario is you finding some smart, rich doctor and realizing what a waste of time I am."

She throws her arms around my neck, holding on so tight, I ain't gotta choice but to wrap my arms 'round her. "Please don't say that," she whispers against my neck. "Please. I love you."

"Love you, too, baby girl."

I use her hair to tug her back so I can see her face again. "She say all this shit outta jealousy or concern?"

Karina only thinks about it for a second. "Concern. But she's a hypocrite too, because she won't stop asking me about Romeo."

Her nose wrinkles in the funniest way when she says my prez's name. I ain't at all bothered that she seems to find him repulsive. On the other hand, I'm real interested to know that her friend's into him.

"Why?"

Karina blushes and looks away before answering. "I don't know. She thinks he's hot for some reason."

Harsh laughter bursts out of me. "Yeah? Feeling might be mutual there."

"He's scary."

"I'm not?"

She reaches out and traces a finger down my cheek and over my bottom lip before answering.

"Not to me."

I take her finger and suck on it. Watch as she goes liquid in my arms. I'm about to lose control, but I still need more information from her. My hands grip her hips, pulling her against me even tighter. "Anything else happen today?"

He gaze darts away. Yup. Thought so.

"It's stupid."

"Nothing that concerns you is stupid. Tell me."

She huffs before meeting my eyes. "Some guy hassled me and Athena." Her mouth tips into a slight smile. "One of your prospects—Cricket?—knocked him out."

"That so?"

"Did you ask him to look after me?"

I shouldn't for one second ever forget how smart my little bitch is. "Maybe. Serves two purposes though." My hand strokes over her cheek, down her neck and right between her tits, tugging the knot in her blouse loose. "Keeps my girl safe. And I need that fucker to graduate in June."

"Oh."

"He's clever, but he ain't book smart."

She cocks her head to the side. "I can tutor him if you want?"

Something about her offer flips my possessive switch. "Why? You like him?"

"No." She blinks and her mouth twists into a distressed little frown that's cute as fuck and makes me feel like an asshole. Her gaze lowers to her lap and she picks at a thread on her skirt. "Just wanted to help."

"I know, baby girl." My fingers tug and pull at her shirt, dragging it down her shoulders and tossing it on the couch. She's left in a bra that barely covers her tits and I tuck the cups down so her fat, pink nipples are on display. I keep my eyes on her face while I cup her tits, rolling her nipple between my fingers, then dipping my head down to take a taste. She smells so fucking sweet and heat comes off her in waves.

"You buy anything else?" I whisper against her ear.

I don't really expect an answer but she nods. "Yes."

"Oh, yeah?"

She scoots out of my lap, surprising me, and runs over to the bags she dropped on the floor when she walked in. I sit back and appreciate the view of her bending over to search through the bags. Christ, she stays like that another second, I'm gonna come in my pants.

I'm not sure what I expected her to return with, but candy wasn't it. Candy she bought specifically for me. All timid like, she holds out the bag. "I thought you'd like them."

Shit, she's fuckin' sweet. It's a small thing. But I can't think of another woman who's bothered to learn anything about me other than how I liked my dick sucked or gave me anything besides the obvious.

I motion for her to climb back in my lap. My fingers twine in her hair, pulling her close for a kiss. Soft trembling lips yield to my mouth and tongue. “Such a sweet girl,” I whisper as I pull away.

Her mouth jerks into a relieved smile. As if, what? She thought I’d be mad at her?

“How much homework you got?”

“None.”

She squeals and wraps her arms around my neck as I lift us off the couch and head upstairs. My hands are full of her ass and I almost send both of us to the floor when she plants kisses on my cheeks and seals her mouth over mine. Somehow, I get us both upstairs and drop her on the bed.

CHAPTER SEVEN

KARINA

"LET ME LOOK AT YOU, beautiful girl."

Excitement pulses through me at Dante's words. I throw my shoulders back, but have trouble meeting his eyes until he places his fingers under my chin tipping my head back.

"Are you my girl?"

"Yes."

"You gonna let me do what I want to you?"

"Yes, daddy."

"I should punish you for hesitating downstairs."

Other girls might be scared. Not me. My pussy's throbbing with anticipation. I squirm as his hands work his belt loose, unable to decide if I want him to tie the belt around my wrists or use it on my ass.

He does neither. Instead, his hands gather my hair into a ponytail that he uses to pull me off the bed. I sink to my knees and he grunts in approval. With jerky movements, he unzips and frees his cock. My eyes stare up and my tongue slicks over my top lip.

"You kill me when you do that, baby girl."

There's no chance to respond. He pulls me into position, the smooth head of his granite-hard cock brushes over my lips and I open immediately to taste him.

He lets out a long hiss. "Your sexy little ass in that outfit has me worked up, baby girl. Need you to make me come, so I can calm down enough to take my time with you."

Sounds perfect to me and I hum with approval while lifting my hands to caress his length.

"Good girl."

I love being his good girl. My nipples harden and ache for his touch. I'm so curious about what he plans to do to me, I open wider when he jams his cock down my throat until I choke.

"Suck me, baby girl."

He said he wants me to suck him, but he's busy holding my head, thrusting in and out the way *he* wants. There isn't much for me to do besides take it.

And I think he likes that the most.

"Look up at me," he barks.

His hard glare softens when I meet his eyes.

"Fuck, Karina," he growls, low enough to make me shiver.

He slows his thrusting and I suck harder, grabbing and rubbing my hands over him the way he's shown me to do so many times.

"Good...good...girl," he gasps, thrusting hard one last time. He comes down the back of my throat so far that I don't taste a thing. I keep sucking and licking as he tries to withdraw until he gasp-laughs. "Easy, baby girl."

When he slips free, I take a few deep breaths and collapse on the floor.

"No. We just started."

I peek up at him and smile. His cock's still glossy with my spit, and my grin widens.

He leans over, lifting me and setting me on the edge of the bed.

"Christ, you're so fuckin' beautiful I don't even know where to start," he says as his gaze roams over every inch of me. The way he sees me makes everything right.

"Will you take your shirt off?"

One corner of his mouth lifts. "You wanna see me?"

"Yes, please."

My tongue slides over my bottom lip as his fingers curl into the hem of his shirt, slowly lifting it over his head. I reach out, then hesitate.

"Touch me, baby girl."

He shuffles closer to the bed so I can trace my fingers over the hard ridges and lines of his abs, up his chest where he captures my hands, bringing them to his mouth. "Love the way you look at me."

I'm not sure what to say, so I wait while he kisses the backs of my hands. "What do you want, Karina?"

"I want to come."

"How?"

"However you want me to."

He ducks his head and mutters a few curses. "Get on all fours."

I turn and scramble into the position he asked. Shiver as he runs his hand over my bare inner thigh. "This is cute, but I'm gonna strip you now."

"Okay," I mumble into the cool sheets beneath my cheek.

There's a tug and the clicking of the cheap zipper. He works the skirt down and I lift one leg after another so he can take if off.

Rough fingers pull my thigh-highs back into position and he cracks his palm against my ass. "Perfect. Go lie on your tummy in the middle of the bed. I'll be right back."

Anticipation flutters in my stomach as I position myself the way he asked. I keep my eyes closed, but sense him pulling the blinds closed. By the sounds, I think he leaves the bedroom for a second. A few drawers open and close, then his hand skims over my ass.

"Lift up."

He slides a towel under me and I squirm from the rush of excitement, wondering what evil things he's planning to do. There's the rustle of his jeans hitting the floor. The bed dips, his leg brushes up against my sensitized skin. Warm, silky liquid dribbles over my lower back and ass. His hands press into my flesh, rubbing in the oil. With aching slowness he works lower, kneading my ass with firm, slow strokes.

"How do you feel, Karina?"

"Excited."

His low chuckle ripples over me. "Not scared?"

"No." Scared? Nope. His fascination with my ass thrills me. It's a small bit of power I seem to hold over Dante. The way he can't get enough of me and wants to own every part of my body. Maybe it's wrong, but I love it.

"I've been neglecting your ass, baby girl."

"I know." I bury my face into the sheets, muffling my

giggles. Dante slaps my ass—hard—and my giggles turn to moans.

"Filthy little bitch," he murmurs.

I wiggle my ass in response, making him laugh. "You like when I play with your ass?"

His hand slaps my cheeks again when I don't respond fast enough. "Yes, Daddy." He groans and I love the sound. Love his laughter, too. Dante's always so controlled and severe. Knowing I crack through his hard exterior, it's the ultimate compliment.

He returns to rubbing my lower back and ass, slowly opening and teasing me. His finger slides down between my cheeks. Barely a whisper at first. He taps my hip. "Arch your ass up."

Wetness gathers between my legs. It's a good thing he laid down a towel first. He groans and grips my ass harder, spreading me wider.

"Oh!" I jump, startled when his tongue flicks over my pussy lips.

His hold tightens. "Stay," he growls. He nibbles and kisses my inner thighs, then runs his tongue flat over my ass. I gasp and almost come from the forbidden sensation. He slides one finger in my pussy and brushes his thumb over my clit. "You like my fingers in your tight little pussy, don't you?"

"God, yes."

He works in another finger, lazily pumping in and out. It feels incredible, but it's not enough to make me come and I whine in frustration.

I get a slap on my pussy, making me jump and moan at the same time.

"Calm yourself, you horny little slut. I plan to take my time with you."

"Oh, fuck. Dante, I want it so bad. Please." I buck my hips against his hand, dying for any bit of pressure to set me off.

His fingers keep working inside of me while his other hand slips around my waist, pulling me up on all fours.

"Ass up. That's fucking beautiful."

His words and his magic fingers send me over the edge. More lube drips into my asshole and before I realize what he's doing, he slips a finger in my behind. "Oh, fuck." The sensation intensifies my orgasm and I'm vaguely aware of tears running down my cheeks.

"Does that hurt?"

"No."

"Good." He slides his fingers out of my pussy but continues stretching my ass. "Do you like that?"

"Yes. You know I do."

"Still need to hear you say it."

"I love everything you do to me. Even when you want to do scary things, I love them."

"Fuck." He leans over and presses a kiss to my forehead. "Thank you, baby girl."

I'm so damn curious and turned on. Dante's been drawing this out forever. Everything he does to me feels good, so I don't think this will be any different. He slides another finger in, gently twisting and stretching. After a few minutes, I feel something thicker and heavier pressing against me.

"This plug's a little bigger than the last one. It's silicone instead of metal, so it should be more comfortable."

"Okay."

"Grab your cheeks and spread them for me, baby girl."

I bite my lip to stop myself from moaning at his dirty request and do as he asks.

"That's beautiful."

The slick head of the plug presses against my ass. Steady pressure. He doesn't stop even when I squeal a little at the intrusion. "Deep breath, baby girl. You can take it. My cock's much bigger."

Oh, God. How am I ever going to take his cock when *this* hurts? But then it's over. The plug's in and I let out a breath. Dante wiggles it around and need throbs through my pussy.

"Stay just like that."

I feel the dip and roll as he gets off the bed. A second later I hear the water in the bathroom running.

When he returns he stands and stares at me for a few seconds. "You're such a good girl, Karina."

"Thank you. Will you please fuck me now?"

Dante

I can't stop laughing at my girl. Ass up in the air. Arms tucked under her. Little purple handle sticking out of her ass. And one hell of a pissy expression on her face.

"Yeah, baby girl. I'm gonna fuck you. With that plug in it's gonna feel like you're getting drilled in both holes." I grab her ankles, twisting and pulling her to the edge of the bed then flipping her onto her back. Spreading her legs like a fucking wishbone, I slam my cock in her and she lets out a short, sharp scream.

"Owwww," she whines.

"Ow? You're soaking fucking wet, baby girl." My thumb finds her clit, rubbing in tight little circles before I start pumping my cock in and out of her. "That better?"

"Y-yes," she pants. "Oh, fuck. Dante, I need to come."

"Already?"

"Yes. Please. Can I?"

Shit, that's fucking hot when she asks in her whining, pleading little girl voice. Fucking amps me up big time. My hand finds the handle of her plug, twisting and tugging just a bit. She goes fucking nuts, writhing on my dick, yelling out my name.

"You like that, baby girl? Feel like you got two dicks up inside you?"

"Yesyesyes."

"Think you'd like that?"

"Oh God, yes."

It's really unfair to ask her questions right now. I think she'd say yes to just about anything in this moment. I fall down over her, sucking her perfect cherry nipples in my mouth.

Soft little uh, and ah sounds fall from her lips. I flick my gaze up and find her watching me. "Can I get on top, please?"

"Fuck, yeah."

She whimpers as I pull out. Because I'm a sadistic fucker when I wanna be, I twist the plug one more time, then slap her ass. She kneels up and waits for me to center myself in the middle of the bed before climbing over me. "Nice and slow, baby girl."

Her face twists into another pissy expression that makes

me want to put her over my knee again. As she's about to sink onto my cock, I grip her hips. "Other way. I wanna play with your ass while you ride me." She stares at me for a second before complying. After rocking up and down on my dick a few times, she glances over her shoulder.

"This isn't working."

It's mean, but her sad kitten pout makes me laugh and I fucking love it when she tells me what she needs instead of faking her way through it. "Come here."

Once she's facing me, my hands cup her tits, thumbs flicking over her nipples. "You're right. Much better."

She's lost though. Too busy riding my cock to give a fuck what I'm saying or doing. With her ass full, she's tighter than fucking hell and it's taking everything I got not to blow.

Thank fuck a few seconds later she screams, pussy throttling my dick. Fire bolts of pleasure shoot down my spine and I'm yelling out my own curses.

She collapses on top of me, breathing hard, licking and kissing my neck.

"You're gonna kill me, baby girl."

Happy humming noises come from her throat as I move her to the side. She snuggles up close, our sweat keeping us glued together. Never thought I'd like this so much. Happy content woman in my arms. No desire to kick her out of my bed. I turn and kiss her forehead. "Let's go wash up."

"Mmmm," she hum-mumbles.

I give her a light squeeze. "You still alive?"

Her eyelids flutter open and she smiles up at me. "I think so."

Most of the time it's my selfish needs driving this relationship. But no woman has ever rocked me the way Karina does. Especially when she slides her hand down her belly, over her pussy and wiggles the way she's doing. "I'm still all tingly down there." The amazement in her voice makes my cock jump.

Fuck me.

Somehow, despite the things she's been through, she's remained somewhat innocent. Even when she says shit like *that.*

I fucking love being the man to show her every filthy thing her body's capable of. I want to do everything imaginable to her. But I also want to *give* her everything I have.

While that's still a new feeling, I'm starting to like it.

CHAPTER EIGHT

KARINA

DANTE'S WEARING such a severe expression when I finally open my eyes. "Did I do something wrong?"

"No, baby girl. Why would you even ask that?"

I don't have an answer, so I bury my face against his chest. His skin is slick with sweat and I tease him with my tongue for a second before he laughs and pulls away.

"Come on, dirty girl. Let's clean you up."

He's not kidding either. I'm thoroughly washed down, lathered up, and rinsed off.

"Hands against the wall."

I turn and wiggle my ass at him before pressing my palms to the slick tile. With teasing slowness he pulls the toy out of my ass, stopping to move it around a few times. Moans fill the air around us and I realize they're coming from me.

"Like that?"

"I think so."

He chuckles close to my ear and I reach back to pull him closer to me.

"What do you want, baby girl?"

My tummy rumbles before I answer.

"I guess that answers my question. My girl needs food."

Keeping one hand on my hip, he twists and shuts the water off.

Back in the bedroom, he slips a T-shirt over my head, and then slides a pair of loose gym shorts on himself before leading me downstairs.

I watch in silence as he prepares a large omelet and toast. "Brinner?" I ask when he sets a plate in front of me.

He raises an eyebrow and I feel silly. "Nothing," I mumble. "Breakfast for dinner? It's something stupid Athena and I used to ask her mom for when we were little."

He stares at me, making me too nervous to eat. "You two been friends a long time?"

"Yeah."

"Get in fights before?"

"We didn't really fight today. She just pissed me off."

I stab into my eggs. Even if Dante keeps watching me with his intense expression, the food smells too good to ignore.

"You said it was because she's concerned."

"Yes. I think so."

"I'm glad your girl's looking out for you."

"You are?"

"Fuck, yeah." He's quiet while he eats, but after a while he catches my eye. "Is she really into Romeo?"

I snort and almost choke on my juice. "Who knows. I think she's just horny and looking to lose her virginity."

Now it's Dante's turn to choke. "Fuck. Jesus, that's a

bad idea. Shit. How's she...you know what? Never mind. Not my concern."

His reaction makes me laugh, because no, I can't imagine Dante wants such intimate details about my best friend.

"So would you say she's like a sister to you?"

"Yes." The word sister puts a damper on our talk and I set my fork down. "I still can't believe I have a sister." I hesitate before asking the thing that's been bugging me since I first learned about Kadence. "Dante, do you think I have more brothers and sisters out there? I mean, my dad's a trucker. If he had my mom and me stashed away here, maybe he has—"

"Christ, baby girl. I hope not." He studies my face for a few seconds. "You really want to meet her?"

A smile tugs at the corners of my mouth. "Oh, yes. I always wanted a sister. I mean, Athena and I are close, but her parents never liked her being friends with me—"

"Why the fuck not?" he barks out, startling me.

My shoulders jerk and I can't meet his eyes. "I don't know. Not good enough for their little princess? Being friends with me is the only thing she's ever stood up to her parents about."

He snorts. "No wonder she wants to fuck Romeo. To piss off Mommy and Daddy."

I'm a terrible friend. Instead of defending Athena, I answer, "Probably."

He shakes his head and collects our plates. When he's finished, he stalks across the room. The look in his eyes tightens my nipples. Naturally he notices and his mouth tips up into a dirty grin. I shift in the stool to face him when he rounds the bar. "Feel better?" he asks in that low, gritty voice that makes me quiver every damn time.

"Yes."

He skims the back of his hand over my cheek. "I like taking care of you, Karina."

Tears prick my eyes and for a second any words are stuck in my throat. "I like you taking care of me."

Turning my stool so my back's up against the bar, he shoves his way between my thighs. His hands settle on my knees and run right up my legs under the T-shirt that's barely covering me as it is. He doesn't strip the shirt off though.

"I can't get enough of you," he rumbles against my ear.

"Will it always be this way?"

He pulls back, staring down at me.

"What way?"

"This." I wave my hand in the small bit of space separating us. "This constant wanting each other?"

A devilish smirk lifts the corners of his mouth. "Will I always be hot to fuck you? Yeah, I think so."

He yanks me closer to the edge of the stool. One of his hands slides up my inner thighs, spreading my legs wider, while his other hand grips the back of my neck, pulling me closer. Firm lips press against mine as he strokes my center. His thumb grazes over my clit and I jump. His hand tightens at the back of my head, keeping our mouths fused together. My breath catches as he pushes two fingers inside me. He breaks our kiss to stare down at where his hand disappears under my shirt. Inside his fingers curve up, rubbing the spot that makes me quiver. My hands wrap around his forearm. Either trying to keep him there or rip his hand away.

"Too much?" he asks.

I babble out a bunch of sounds before I find the word I'm looking for. "No."

His lips trail over my jaw, nip my earlobe.

"Let's go back upstairs," he whispers.

Dante

After our shower and dinner break, damn fucking right I lead my girl right back upstairs. Her cheeks flush bright pink when I strip her out of her T-shirt.

"Lie back on the bed for me, baby girl."

She blinks a few times, her tits heaving as her breathing speeds up. But then she's on her back, looking unsure and uncomfortable. I'm a sick fucker, because her discomfort warms the blood rushing straight to my cock.

"What are you doing?" she asks in a shaky little voice.

"Gonna shave your pretty pussy bald," I answer as I walk into the bathroom to gather some supplies.

"I'm sorry," she calls out.

"What for?"

She doesn't answer until I'm back in the room with a towel, cup of water, shaving cream and shiny new razor. "For not keeping up on it. I know you like—"

"Karina. Nothing to be sorry for. I'm shaving your pussy because it's mine and I feel like it."

"Oh. Okay."

"I want to be the one who does everything to you."

Her big blue eyes stare up at me and her lips part.

"And sticking my face in your snatch for the next twenty minutes or so isn't exactly a hardship."

Those filthy words make her giggle and the sound turns my mouth up into a grin. Never smiled as much as I have since she came into my life.

"Feet flat on the bed, baby girl."

She's quick to comply and it only gets my dick harder. Concentrating is going to be a challenge. "Spread your legs nice and wide."

This time she's slow. Why, I have no idea since I've been up in her cunt so many God damn times it isn't even funny. I take my sweet ass time massaging her skin, spreading cream over her short hairs. Basically turning this into foreplay rather than simple grooming. She gasps and squirms, but keeps her legs open.

"Good girl," I whisper. "Don't move, okay?"

She lifts her head, staring down at me, and nods.

My hand's steady and the razor glides over her carefully, even so, she giggles. The purest, sweetest sound that makes me feel like one dirty motherfucker.

And gets me harder than steel.

"Don't move, baby girl. Not even laughing."

"I'm trying, but it tickles," she sighs.

She barely takes a breath as I shave right toward her virgin ass.

"Dante?" she whispers.

"Yes?"

"Will you please fuck me when you're done?"

Jesus Christ.

"Yeah, baby. I'm gonna fuck you. First I'm gonna put my mouth all over your bare skin. Then I'll fuck you nice and slow for a bit before pounding you hard until you're screaming my name."

She doesn't respond, so I glance up and find her playing with her nipples.

"Like that?" I ask.

"Oh, yes."

CHAPTER NINE

DANTE

ROMEO CALLS me in again the next morning. This time Karina's father's visiting the clubhouse when I arrive. Motherfucker. I want to smash my fist through his mouth every time I see the stupid fuck.

My prez pulls me aside when he sees me. "We may have worked out a solution. So don't mention your offer to pay off the debt."

I wasn't aware I'd formally offered to pay anything off. The stare I give Romeo before nodding seems to communicate that because he smirks before leading me into one of the spare meeting rooms.

Tucker stands and holds out his hand, which I ignore, before dropping into a chair opposite him. I ain't sittin' anywhere near Tucker. Not sure I'll be able to stop myself from killin' him.

"I wanna make things right with you, Romeo," Tucker snivels like a kid caught stealing from a candy jar. "Got some cash coming my way—"

"I know you're good for it, Tucker," Romeo says in a

slow, grave tone. "I got a run I need you on. I'll forgive half the debt if you can do it."

Tucker gives Romeo a wary look and I don't blame him. Whatever Romeo needs is probably risky. But it ain't like Tucker takes care of his family. Something happens to him, he won't be missed.

Once they work out those details, Romeo tips his head my way. Gotta give my prez credit, he knows I got all sorts of questions for Tucker. As much as Romeo pisses me off sometimes, I appreciate that he made sure I was here for this sit-down.

"How's Karina?" Tucker asks.

Fucker's got nerve. I'll give him that. "Like you give a shit."

He opens his mouth again, but I hold up a hand. "Don't. Let's not pretend you give a fuck about her. She's my responsibility now. If she wants to see you, I ain't stoppin' her. But otherwise, leave her the fuck alone."

His eyes widen and he swallows hard. It's killin' this asshole to have to sit there and take attitude from me—the guy fucking his daughter. Yeah, Tucker's hung out at our clubhouse once or twice. He knows all the dirty shit that goes down inside these walls. Too fuckin' bad.

"You *are* gonna get me her sister's contact information though."

"Dante, I can't do that—"

"I ain't asking, motherfucker. Your other daughter doesn't know about Karina? I suggest you sit down and have a nice little father-daughter chat with her. *Soon.* Karina wants to meet her sister."

Tucker twitches and looks to Romeo. He ain't gonna

find any help there. Romeo keeps his eyes on me and nods for me to go ahead.

"You have until Karina's graduation. I don't want anything upsetting or distracting her from finishing up—"

"How's she doing? In school, I mean?" Tucker asks.

I drill him with a *Shut the fuck up* stare, but answer his question. Not because he deserves the answer, but because I'm proud of my girl. Proud of how fuckin' smart she is. Proud of how well she's doing in school despite this piece of shit across from me not doing *his* job.

"She's near the top of her class. No thanks to you."

"Good. That's good."

"Yeah, you owe him. Dante's planning to send your daughter to college," Romeo says with a smirk. Guess that's still bothering him. Dick's way too up in my business. What happens between me and my ol' lady isn't really his concern.

Tucker looks anything but grateful. No, the expression on his face says he's afraid I'm gonna ask for money from his deadbeat ass.

Fuck that.

"She still want to be a doctor?" Tucker asks.

"She's thinking about it."

"Her momma always told her that was a stupid idea."

Sounds like her mom was as useless as Tucker, which is tragic but it makes me even prouder of my girl. "Karina's got a mind of her own."

Romeo snorts and I slowly turn my head his way.

"Please. You got that bitch wrapped so tight around your dick, it's amazing you can walk."

Whether he said that to fuck with me or Tucker, I'm

not sure. My jaw works and something in my stare makes Romeo uncomfortable, because he sits up. "No disrespect to Karina. She's good ol' lady material. Knows her place. Gonna be a fine asset to the club when Dante formally claims her."

Tucker almost chokes. Because, yeah, he knows how an ol' lady gets claimed in our club. Romeo smirks. I ain't real good at this whole "meet the parents" weirdness we seem to be doing. Beyond that, I'm not so stupid I don't get how fucked up this whole situation is.

"Give me until the weekend. Let me talk to Kadence," Tucker says. "If she's okay with meeting Karina, I'll help you set it up."

"Don't make me hunt down your other daughter on my own, Tucker." He flinches, because yeah he was already plotting how to get out of doing this. "Let's be clear, Karina is my *only* concern in this situation. I don't give a fuck if it makes you uncomfortable to explain to your other daughter what a low life piece of shit you are. Man the fuck up for once in your life. Otherwise I'm gonna do it for you. How do you think that turns out?"

The color drains from his face. "Don't hurt her."

What the fuck's wrong with this guy? "I ain't gonna *hurt* anyone, you prick. They both deserve to know the truth and to have a relationship if they want it."

"Can we dial back the Dr. Phil bullshit?" Romeo asks. "Tucker, get my shit delivered on time with no complications. That's your first priority. Then you need to handle your family business. Don't forget, I got a straight line to the Savage Dragon's prez. Ain't gonna take me a minute to track Kadence down and hand over the information to Dante."

Tucker stares at his hands in defeat. "Fine. Kadence is... a little wild though. If Karina's really serious about her studies, Kadence might not be the best influence."

"That's *my* problem, motherfucker. Not yours. Just do what you're told," I growl at him.

After Tucker leaves, Romeo settles back in his chair. "Damn, brother. You almost brought tears to my eyes. Why do you give a fuck about Karina meeting her half-sister? Sounds as if she'll be a bad influence on your girl."

He's fucking with me, so I don't give his question any consideration. "We done here, prez?" I ask as I stand.

Sadie's at the bar in the main room and Romeo heads straight for her. I follow so I can talk to her for a second.

"You see Cricket outside, Sadie-girl?"

She nods, even though Romeo's got his hand down the front of her shirt, pawing at her tits like he hasn't been laid in weeks. She gives me an odd look as if she, I don't know what, expects me to join in?

Fuck that. I can honestly say I've got zero interest.

She turns to face Romeo, and they both ignore me.

"You want me to run and get Cricket?" Melody asks from behind the bar. She's a newer girl, and I've barely ever spoken to her.

"Thanks, sweetheart."

Couple minutes later, Romeo and Sadie have moved their session to a couch in the corner and Cricket's at my back.

"You wanted to talk to me, Dante?"

I turn and give the kid a serious assessment. Unlike

some of our prospects, he doesn't flinch when I stare him down. Even when I don't speak right away he stands tall, waiting for instruction.

"Sit."

Surprised, his gaze darts to Melody and then back to me before he slides onto the stool next to me.

"Heard you were looking after my girl yesterday?"

A flash of relief crosses his face, before he goes stone cold again. "Oh, yeah. Ain't nothin'."

"Did I ask you to look after her?"

Now he's confused, but I'm curious to see how he'll respond. "Not really, sir. But uh, the guy I hit called her a whore, and I don't care to hear anyone disrespect a girl like that. You know, unless she's into that sort of thing." He flashes a dirty smile at me and winks at Melody.

Cocky little fucker.

But I like his answer.

"Good. You share any classes with Karina?"

"Just one—Accounting. She's in a lot of advanced classes."

Sounds like my girl. "How're you doing in that class?"

"Uh, it's the only one I'm doing well in besides gym and Auto Tech."

"Define 'doing well.'"

"I dunno. B average right now."

"You gonna make it to graduation?"

"I think so. Having a little trouble with English Lit. Lots of boring shit we gotta read and analyze."

"All right. Karina will tutor you if you think you need it."

He seems surprised. "Okay."

"I don't think I need to explain what will happen if you lay one finger on her, do I?"

"No, Dante. I wouldn't...I mean, not that she isn't...uh, never. No, sir."

I clench my jaw so I don't end up laughing. "Good. Get back to work outside."

He slides off the stool and lopes out of the clubhouse.

"That's sweet, Dante," Melody says. Forgot she'd been listening in. She bats her long eyelashes at me, but I ignore the invitation she's obviously extending.

"Fuck, you are whipped," Romeo says, slapping my back. A glance over my shoulder shows me Sadie's long gone.

"Thought you were saving yourself for Karina's friend?" I ask, because I can be an asshole, too.

He laughs and shakes his head. "Thought she was off-limits?"

"As if anything's off-limits to you." Here's where I should probably inform him of Athena's virgin status. But I feel like that's a tidbit of information he should learn all on his own. Preferably after he fucks her and she's clinging to him like seaweed.

Hey, I've never pretended to be anything other than a prick.

"Sadie's been lonely since you gave her the brush-off," he informs me while he finishes buckling his belt.

"Please, Sadie hasn't been lonely one day since she set foot in this clubhouse."

"No, but fuck she gives good head."

I shrug because now all I can picture is *Karina's* mouth wrapped around my cock.

Karina

"I'm sorry about yesterday," Athena says as soon as she sees me at school.

I don't answer right away. Not because I'm still mad. I'm just not sure what to say.

"Please, please, please don't be mad at me."

"I'm not."

"Good. You know I just worry about you, right?"

"I know," I sigh. Couldn't stay mad at Athena if I wanted to.

We decide to eat lunch outside in a corner of the stone patio seniors are allowed to use.

"Why so quiet today?" I ask after she finishes her sandwich.

Her face pulls into a miserable frown. Very unlike Athena. "My parents found out I didn't apply anywhere and they're livid."

"You didn't apply *anywhere*? Not even in California?" Is she nuts?

"No. I want to give this acting thing a serious chance, not do half school, half acting."

"Athena, you have to—"

"No," she says, cutting me off. "I swear I have a plan. I'm going to give it two years. If I haven't made it by then, I'll go to college."

"Athena—"

"Come on, Karina. College can wait *two years*."

"Okay. But what are you going to live on? There's no way your parents will support you if you're not in school."

Her mouth twists into a sour expression. "No. But I've been saving for years."

Again, I feel crappy that I didn't know this about my best friend.

"Aren't you scared to go live in a new place all by yourself?"

She gives me a curious look. "No. I'm excited to see new things. I won't be alone. I've been chatting online with another girl. We're going to get an apartment together."

"Are you nuts? It's probably some creepy old dude."

Her eye-roll tells me how serious she's taking my concern. "I'll be fine."

My phone buzzes and I get a flutter of excitement thinking it might be Dante. Every now and then he sends me sweet texts letting me know I'm on his mind.

It's not Dante though.

"What is it?" Athena asks, as I scroll through the e-mail. "Oh, that volunteer job at the hospital wants me to come in for an interview tomorrow."

Her nose wrinkles. "Volunteer? Why do they need to interview you? Shouldn't they just be grateful anyone wants to work for free?"

That's how Athena's mind works. "They probably want to make sure I'm not some freak. Shit, I don't have any interview-y type clothes."

"You can borrow something from my closet. Or we can go to the mall after school."

I glance at her slim hips and decide nothing in her closet is going to fit over my fat ass. We're not twelve anymore and I've filled out a lot more than Athena has. "I don't think I can fit into your stuff anymore."

She glances down at her chest. "Way to remind me I have the figure of an eight-year-old boy."

We giggle together, much like we did when we were twelve. While she's slender—willowy, some talent agent might tell her soon—there's nothing boyish about her.

After school, we head to the mall. It feels familiar and I'm glad we're on better terms today. Athena's helpful with this stuff and we quickly pick out a modest dress and sweater-cardigan. "You can't wear, like a suit or something. It has to be age-appropriate," she cautions me.

"Got it. Thanks. Maybe you should try out for one of those 'learn how to dress yourself' reality shows when you're in Hollywood."

She snicker-snorts at my sarcasm.

We part in the parking lot with a hug. "Call me later?" she asks.

Dante's bike's waiting in the driveway. I love all this extra time he's been spending here lately. It's nice not to come home to an empty house.

"Hey, baby girl. Where you been?" he asks when I walk in the door.

"Shopping." He raises an eyebrow and I hold up the bags. "The hospital scheduled me for an interview and education session tomorrow and I didn't have anything interview worthy."

"That's great." His mouth turns up in a genuine smile and my heart races at his encouraging voice.

"The program's only two days a week, but at least I'll learn some stuff."

"Sounds good. You get registered for the class, yet?"

Since my parents never bothered with my school stuff, it's weird to have to answer to someone about these things. But also nice. "Not yet. I want to have my schedule straightened out and talk to my adviser again."

"Good." He motions me to come sit next to him and I set my bags down before approaching. "I spoke to Cricket today. He's officially keeping an eye on you."

I chuckle at the image of Dante terrorizing poor Cricket into watching over me at school.

"He's having some trouble in English, so if you can help him out, I'd appreciate it."

"Sure. Do you know who he has?"

"No fuckin' clue."

"That's okay. I'll talk to him tomorrow."

Dante nods, but a sterner expression moves over his face. "I warned him what would happen if he made a move on you."

I can't help the snort that comes out of me. "I'm sure you did."

"I spoke to your father today," he says without easing me into the conversation.

"Did he ask about me?" I hate how pathetic and needy I sound.

Dante doesn't make me feel bad about it though. His face softens and he pulls me closer. "Yeah. He did. Told him how smart you are and how well you're doing in school." He bites his lip as if he's holding back the less savory parts of their talk.

"And?"

"I told him he's gonna get me your sister's number so you two can meet."

"You did? Oh my God. Thank you. When?"

He holds up a hand. "After graduation." When I open my mouth to protest he shakes his head.

"Listen, I know you're excited to have a sister and you're dying to meet her. But, I want you to consider the possibility that she won't feel the same way."

The thought had occurred to me once or twice, but I kept pushing it away. Now I need to take a minute to picture our family "reunion" a different way.

Dante nods as if he reads my thoughts.

"Did my father say she's upset?"

"He said a lot of stupid, useless things. But no. It's just human nature. It's gonna be a big shock for her, too, don't forget."

That's true.

"So that's why I don't want you to think about it until after you're done with school, okay? I don't want you getting your feelings hurt and it messing up your grades or anything."

I can't swallow over the lump in my throat. Instead I fling my arms around him and bury my face against his chest. His big, strong arms squeeze me back. "You're not mad?" he asks.

"No. Thank you for looking out for me."

"Always, baby girl."

CHAPTER TEN

KARINA

THE NEXT WEEK somehow goes by fast and seems to drag at the same time. The school handed out five "official" invitations to each graduating senior to pass out to friends and family.

"God, these are hideous." Athena wrinkles her nose at the garish red and green cards that match our school colors. "They look like Rudolph took a shit on them or something."

I choke and sputter with laughter. "You're disgusting."

"Nothing like waiting until the last minute to invite someone."

"I guess they figure everyone important should already know about it? Who cares. I just want to get the fuck out of here."

"Me too."

It's finals week, so classes are sporadic. Dante's been on a run and I suspect it has more to do with wanting me to study than club business. Luck or Cricket have been coming by the house to check on me. Last night I stayed over at Athena's much to her mother's distress.

I'm not ashamed to say I made dinner especially awkward when I let it slip I'd been accepted into State's pre-med program. Oh, and then I casually mentioned my summer job and my volunteer position at the hospital. It's not that I wanted to make Athena look bad, but I'm tired of her parents' judgmental attitude toward me. They still act as if I'm not good enough to hang around their daughter. I'd always ignored it before, but since I'm feeling a little more confident these days, it feels good to brag a little.

Thankfully Athena's not mad at me. She thought her mother's uptight congratulations was as amusing as I did.

I'm treated to the surprise of Dante's bike in the driveway when I arrive home. He opens the front door and I fly into his arms.

"Fuck, I missed you, baby girl," he says as he lifts me off the ground.

"I missed you, too," I say between kisses.

There are not a whole lot of words after that. There *is* a lot of naked, bent over the living room couch sex though.

Dante

"Dante, should I invite my father to my graduation?"

Lying in bed after fucking the hell out of Karina is just about the last place I want to talk about her deadbeat father.

"Why're you asking?"

"We got these official invites at school. For family guests. Should I give him one? Do you think he'll come?"

"I don't know, baby girl. But if you want him there, give it to him."

She chews on her thumbnail a little—something she almost never does. I grasp her hand, pulling it away from her mouth "You need to put something in your mouth, I'll give you my cock."

"Already done that," she sasses back.

"No rule saying you can't do it again."

Her bare thigh rubs against mine and she rolls to her side, facing me. "What's wrong?" I ask after she stares at me for a few minutes.

"Nothing. I'm just happy you're home."

"Me too. What do you have going on tomorrow?"

"Morning at the library and I have an exam in the afternoon."

"Okay. I'll be at the clubhouse most of the day if you need me."

"Thanks." She hesitates again. "Do you know if my dad's home?"

"No idea. Wanna give him a call?"

"I was thinking of driving over there and giving him the invitation in person."

Fucking hell. Driving over to that deadbeat's house is the last thing I feel like doing. "Okay. Get dressed. I'll take you now before it gets much later."

"You don't have to—"

She stops mid-sentence when she takes in the look on my face.

NATURALLY, the douche isn't home. "What do you want to do?" I ask. Karina's old key doesn't work anymore. Amazing how the prick had time to change the locks but can't pick up a fucking phone to call his daughter.

She taps the envelope against her hand a few times before answering. "I guess I'll leave it under the door and give him a call to let him know it's here?"

"Sounds good."

I didn't expect her to whip out her phone and call him right this second, but that's what she does. Leaves him a voicemail with all the information that's in the invite. Well, at least the asshole has no excuse for not showing up.

"Do you think he's mad we're together?" she asks as we walk back to my bike.

"Don't give a fuck if he is. No one's gonna keep us apart. I'll destroy anyone who gets in my way, even him. You're mine."

I didn't mean to get so intense, but the thought of that man always manages to piss me off.

"I like being yours," she says.

Good.

"Mind if we stop by the clubhouse? I'll ask Romeo if he knows what your dad's up to."

"Sure."

For a weeknight, the clubhouse is pretty busy. Fuck only knows what Romeo will say in front of Karina, so I park her little ass at the bar next to Sadie. "Keep an eye on her?"

"No problem." Sadie nods.

Karina doesn't seem too thrilled about the arrangement, but she doesn't protest.

I take off in search of my prez.

Kind of wish I hadn't found him in such a compromising position with Amy, but when they're done, she leaves.

"Christ, can't you go two minutes without getting one of those bitches on their knees?"

He snorts. "You come here for a reason, or to give me shit? Don't be jealous because you're getting bored with the same old pussy."

Bored isn't the word I'd use to describe what Karina and I have. But that ain't any of his business. The less he knows, or thinks he knows about us, the better.

"You hear from Tucker lately?"

"Yeah. Sent him back down to the border on another run."

"Seriously?"

"He needs me to clear that debt and I need someone who doesn't look connected to us, since Hemi's fuck-up. Why you looking for him?"

"One, it's almost time for him to get me that fucking number for Karina's sister. Two, she wants to invite the asshole to her graduation. She dropped off an invite at his house, but I want to make sure he knows about it."

"Why?"

"Because I don't want her disappointed."

"He's a piece of shit. Thought you'd want him far away from her."

My shoulders lift. What the fuck do I know about any of this? "He's still her dad. She should have what little family she's got there."

"You're getting soft." He chuckles. "So when is graduation?"

That kicks off my radar. "Why?"

"Because apparently this club's her family now. Maybe some of us should be there."

It would be a nice sentiment if I didn't know the real reason he wants to tag along. I don't even bother trying to hold in my laughter. "You fucking serious?"

"Why not.?" He shrugs. "We got two prospects graduating, too."

"Yeah, and an almost-legal chick you wanna sink your dick in."

"Well, that, too." He tones down the dirty smirk-face. "You know if she's got a boyfriend?"

"Like it matters?"

"No, I guess not."

"I don't think so. From what Karina says, her friend's pretty sheltered." That's putting it mildly.

His eyes light up like the dirty pussy-loving pervert he is. "Fuck. They're always the dirtiest girls."

"You would know."

Karina

Hanging out with Sadie isn't too horrible. I mean, I know she's fucked Dante in the past, which is a little uncomfortable, but she's always been nice to me. Unlike this other catty bitch, Melody, who I'm pretty sure graduated from my high school last year.

As soon as Sadie leaves to check on something, Melody pounces. "You know your man hooks up when you're in school, right?"

She says *school* with a bitchy wrinkled-nose face. I'm tempted to tell her how ugly that face makes her look, but I don't.

"I highly doubt that," I answer in a bored voice. I'm proud to say that isn't a lie either. I trust Dante.

"Not me," she says in a rush as if she's trying to be my best friend all of a sudden. "Just the other day, your *friend* Sadie blew him on the couch." Damn, I really hate girls who love doing nothing but starting drama and trouble.

"You know, Melody," I say with a long, dramatic pause. "Maybe if you spent this much effort on your own life, you wouldn't be such a miserable twat."

Behind me, Sadie's laughter rings out. "Good one, Karina. I was about to say something not quite as classy."

She settles her hand on my shoulder and stands next to me. "Stop trying to fuck with her. Dante will kick your skinny little ass right out the door if you upset his girl."

Melody *sticks her tongue out* at me—what are we, five?

"Melody," Romeo snaps. "Go do something useful somewhere else."

I turn to find Romeo and Dante in the doorway to the club's "chapel room." Dante lifts his chin. His way, I think, of asking if I'm okay. I nod and he goes back to his conversation with Romeo.

Sadie hops onto the barstool next to me. "You did good.

Don't ever be afraid to stick up for yourself around these bitches. You're gonna be Dante's old lady. Everyone knows it."

"Uh—"

"Club whores, hell even some of the old ladies will try to test you to see what you're made of."

"Why?"

"That's the way it is." She tilts her head to the side. "I think you can handle it."

"Thanks." I sound more confused than thankful but she accepts my words.

"Just so you know, Melody was lying her ass off. Dante hasn't looked at another girl since you. Not even me, and we used to be pretty regular—"

I throw my hand up in a stop gesture a couple inches from her face. "I really don't need details."

She flashes a quick, apologetic smile. "Sorry. He's smitten with you, that's all."

Smitten. Odd word to use to describe Dante and I let out a chuckle.

Sadie laughs, too. "Right? Who could imagine big, bad Dante as a smitten kitten?" she says, sending both of us into a fit of silly giggles.

When we catch our breath, I look her over. "Are you mad that he didn't want you as his old lady?" That's a pretty obnoxious question for me to ask, but I can't help it. I can't figure Sadie out.

"Hell, no." She glances around the packed clubhouse. "This life isn't for me long-term. Besides, I've fucked almost every brother in this charter, so never gonna happen."

"Wow. Okay then."

She shrugs. "I like sex and I *don't* like commitment. This is the perfect place if you keep your expectations to a minimum. Girls like Melody who come here hoping to snag an ol' man just end up bitter little bitches."

I have no words, but for some reason I really appreciate Sadie's directness.

Thick, tattooed forearms wrap around my middle. Dante. I relax against him and he kisses my cheek. "You okay?" he whispers in my ear.

"Yeah. Sadie was keeping me company." I reach over and squeeze her hand in thanks.

He dips his chin to acknowledge Sadie, but doesn't say anything else. Romeo, on the other hand, wraps his arm around Sadie's waist. "How do you feel about high school graduations, Sadie?"

Behind me, Dante groans. Sadie seems confused for a minute. "Haven't been to one since my own," she finally says.

"Well, our girl Karina here is graduating Friday afternoon, and since she doesn't have a lot of family, Dante and I thought some of her Iron Bulls family should be there."

That sounds like a load of crap if I ever heard one, but I keep my face neutral. "You don't have to do that, Romeo. It'll be so boring."

"Sure," Sadie answers slowly, throwing me an *Is that okay with you?* face.

"Good," Romeo says, as if he's somehow done his good deed for the day. He tugs Sadie off her stool and the two of them disappear down the hall.

"What was that all about?" I ask Dante as he takes Sadie's vacant seat.

"No fucking idea. I tried to talk him out of it. Figure he's either hoping to see your friend or he's sincere and trying to make up for giving me so much shit."

"Shit about what?"

His mouth flattens into a thin line, as if he wishes he hadn't said so much.

"He's just jealous of my hot lil' girl."

Luck joins us before I question Dante further. Romeo returns without Sadie and claps Luck on the back. "Perfect. You can join us at Karina's graduation, too."

Luck's gaze roams over me for a brief second before he seems to come to a decision. "Ah, sure, prez. Dante, that okay with you?"

This is all getting too weird for me. Dante interprets my pleading look correctly and takes my hand, sliding me off the stool. "We're heading out. You hear anything, let me know, prez."

"Will do."

Finally the bizarre night at the biker compound is over.

CHAPTER ELEVEN

DANTE

No surprise Karina hasn't heard from her dad. First thing Monday morning looks like I'll be tracking him down and beating some information out of him. Not even a phone call on her graduation day. He's gonna get a few extra punches just for hurting my girl's feelings.

Karina shakes it all off. She did well on all of her exams —not that I expected anything different.

"I don't know why I bothered. No one will see my dress when it's covered by the hideous gowns we have to wear," she grumbles as she checks herself out in the bathroom mirror.

"You look beautiful, baby girl."

"Thank you."

"Come here."

She rushes over and wraps her arms around my waist careful not to touch her made up face to my T-shirt. "Ready to go?"

"Yes. I told Athena I'd meet her in front of the school at eleven."

We take my truck to the school. The place is jumping today. Crazed teenagers and proud parents everywhere. I feel like a creepy motherfucker here to watch my girlfriend graduate from high school. Then she smiles at me and I shake it off. Never gave a fuck what anyone thought of me before. Ain't gonna start now.

Athena squeals and runs over almost knocking Karina down with her enthusiastic greeting. They talk so fast I can't make out their words. Most of it sounds like "I can't believe we're finally getting out of here."

"Where're your parents?" Karina asks.

"Inside. Is your dad coming?"

Karina's mouth turns down and if it wasn't for Athena looking just as upset as my girl, I'd be pissed at her for upsetting Karina.

"Fuck him, Karina," Athena says with a sassy chin-lift. "You kicked ass this year."

Damn, I like this little bitch sometimes.

I almost groan when I spot Romeo approaching our group. Correction, Romeo *and* Sadie.

Athena's eyes narrow as she follows my gaze. "Who's that?" she asks, poking Karina in the ribs.

"Romeo. I think you've met him," Karina answers with a straight face, making me chuckle.

"Don't be a bitch."

Sadie runs up and hugs Karina—wasn't aware they were so close. "Congratulations, sweetie."

"Thanks."

Luck joins us next and gives Karina a brief hug while also congratulating her. My girl seems a little overwhelmed from all the attention.

"Athena and I have to go line up with our class." She waves the four envelopes she's holding in the air and then hands one to each of us. "You'll need these to get in."

"You really didn't have to come," I remind Romeo once the girls leave. He shrugs. "Prospects worked hard, too. Might as well support 'em."

What a load of bullshit.

"Wolf and his old lady are coming, too," he says as if he knows I'm calling him a liar in my head. But it doesn't surprise me our VP would show up. He's also worked closely with the prospects and his ol' lady is a mother hen type if ever there was one.

We finally go inside and find Wolf. Bunch of squares give us some dirty looks. As if bikers shouldn't be at a high school graduation.

The first person who asks me if Karina's my daughter gets knocked the fuck out.

CHAPTER TWELVE

KARINA

ATHENA and I begged and pleaded with the kid who was sitting between us to swap seats. He finally agreed. She clasps my hand as the ceremony starts and we titter throughout all the speeches. It came down to two missed questions on my history final that knocked me out of second place. I'm more than okay with not having to speak today.

Instead, I hold my best friend's hand and wonder where we'll be in six months...a year...ten years from now. This big trip she's planning to California still scares me even though she's promised to call and text so much I won't even know she's gone.

I doubt that.

I'm nervous about all the things I have planned for the summer. Upset that my father's not here. Anxious about maybe getting to meet my sister soon.

Before I know it, we're called on stage to accept our diplomas. Our Vice Principal, Mr. Hacket, excuses himself when they get to the Rs. I chuckle under my breath. Guess he's still scared of Dante.

Dante.

He said he has something special planned for me tonight and something important to discuss with me tomorrow. I'm dying to find out what those things are.

I must space out because suddenly, Athena's jamming her elbow in my ribs and shouting in my ear. "We're free! We're finally free!"

We hug a few people we've stayed friends with. I even find Cricket and even give him a big hug. He looks terrified —as if Dante might pop out at any moment and beat him to death for touching me.

Athena and I run into her parents first. I'm scanning the crowd for Dante. Or my dad. Dante's so big he should be easy to spot. I'm looking in the wrong direction though, because he surprises me by coming up behind me and sweeping me up into his arms and kissing me deep.

"So proud of you baby girl," he whispers against my lips before setting me down.

I twine my hand with his to keep myself upright, then face Athena's shocked parents.

Oops.

I introduce them to Dante *and* Romeo, which is awkward as hell. Her parents aren't even subtle about hustling Athena away from us. Athena turns and wiggles her fingers at us like a beauty queen riding a parade float.

"Am I that terrifying?" Romeo asks with a snicker.

I snort and shake my head. "Don't take it personally. They've never liked me either."

Romeo pats my arm in an awkward way that's similar

to how you pat a cute little purse-dog. "Congrats, girl. Your man wouldn't shut the fuck up about you being third in the class."

He almost sounds sincere, and I look to Dante who shrugs.

"Where did Luck and Sadie go?" I ask.

Dante points toward the parking lot. "Our VP and his ol' lady were here, too. I think they're heading back to the clubhouse with the prospects."

"You can join us, Karina," Romeo says. He glances at Dante after making the offer. Some unspoken communication bounces between them. Can't be anything good. Dante grips my hand tighter and we leave the school together.

It's barely three in the afternoon, but the clubhouse is wild when we get there. Dante's look of disgust speaks volumes as he helps me down from his truck. "Fuckin' prospects are gonna think it's always like this," he grumbles. "Don't say anything, but Cricket and Buttons are getting patched in tomorrow."

"That's awesome. I know Cricket was really nervous about what would happen after graduation."

"Well, club's still gotta vote it, but I don't think anyone will vote no." He places a hand on either side of my face and backs me up against the truck. "Now. The rest of the night is all about *you*," he murmurs as he trails kisses down my neck. "And tomorrow and the next day," he continues. "Got a lot of time to make up for."

"Thank you for letting me study all week," I whisper as I spread my hand over his crotch. "Oh, you *did* miss me."

"Don't fuck with me, baby girl. I'm so torqued up I'm

about to have you blow me in this parking lot to take the edge off."

"I can do that."

He snatches my hand away and pulls me inside. "I think I'm gonna put you over my knee first," he says against my ear.

The saucy reply on the tip of my tongue evaporates when I spot my father hanging out with Melody inside.

CHAPTER THIRTEEN

DANTE

What the fuck?

One minute I'm about to strip her out of her dress in the middle of the main room and give her a preview of what a club claiming's all about. The next she's shaking like a leaf, tears threatening to fall from her big blue eyes.

Someone's gonna die.

My gaze lands on Tucker and rage clouds my vision. This motherfucker never responded to her invitation. Didn't show the fuck up to her graduation. Now he's got the nerve to be in my clubhouse, messing around with a girl not much older than his daughter?

Fuck no.

I storm over and his guilty eyes stare up at me in confusion. Drunk. The asshole's drunk at three in the afternoon. Melody takes one look at my raging face, squeaks and runs away.

"Dad?"

"Hey, Karina." He flashes a goofy grin. "Today was the big day, right?"

"You know it was. Why weren't you there? I tried calling you. I tried—"

He has the nerve to point at me. "He told me to stay away from you."

"You shifty motherfucker. Don't you dare put it on me." Is he out of his God damn mind? He knows my role in the club. Knows I can kill him with my bare fucking hands.

Next to me, Karina trembles like a timid kitten. Or so I think, when I glance down at her it's clear she's pissed. "I'm done. Dante, can we go *home* please?" She turns her back on her father and takes my hand.

Before we leave, I lean over and get in Tucker's face. "This isn't over. I better have Kadence's phone number and address by Monday morning or life's gonna get real unpleasant for you." I keep my voice low and full of menace designed to send a clear message.

"Romeo—"

"I don't give a fuck what Romeo told you," I snap before he even gets the stupid thought out. "You think he's gonna protect your ass forever, you're wrong. You ain't a brother."

How dire this situation is seems to be sinking into his alcohol-addled brain. "I'm her father. You won't kill me. She'll hate you."

"I doubt that."

Outside, the sun stabs us in the eyes and Karina lifts her arm to shield her face.

"Where to, baby girl?"

"Home."

When we're in the truck and I got the A/C running, I

turn and take her hand. "I set something up for you tonight. But now I don't—"

"Anything to take my mind off things."

Well, what I had planned will definitely do *that*.

I'm gonna have to give her some warning and see if she's still up for it.

She trudges up the stairs when we get home and I have no idea how to make her feel better in a way that doesn't include fucking her.

Upstairs I hear her running a bath and I go up to find her sitting in the tub. Naked, beautiful, hair pulled up into a messy little knot that I want to put my hand around and use to guide her mouth to my dick.

"You okay?"

She leans back, giving me a perfect view of her breasts and my dick responds immediately.

"I feel better now." She opens her eyes. "Dante?" her soft questioning voice has an edge of need.

"Yeah, baby girl?"

"Will you finally fuck my ass tonight?"

Jesus Christ. That was the last thing I expected out of her. Laughter explodes from me, but she's totally serious. "Later tonight. Got another size up plug I want to see if your ass can handle."

Her mouth curves into a dreamy smile and she sits up, wrapping her arms around her legs and laying her cheek on her knees. "Will you come in my ass or on my back?"

Motherfucker, all these innocently-asked filthy questions are doing a number on my dick. He's screaming to get out.

"Don't know. Think I'll decide in the moment." I let

her sit for a few more minutes. “Come on, you’ve been in there long enough.”

I help her up out of the tub and dry her off before taking her hand and leading her into the bedroom. Without any words, she tugs at my shirt, stripping it off me. Her little hands go for my belt and jeans next. She sinks down to the floor, tugging everything off and tossing it in a pile in the corner. Waiting patiently for whatever I’m about to ask of her, she stares up at me.

My hand twines into her hair, holding on to her messy little bun like a handle and steering her to my cock. Eager, she opens her mouth and takes me to the back of her throat.

“Fuuuuck.” Her warm, wet tongue flicks over me perfectly. She sucks deeper and I’m unable to form a single thought. I let myself fall into the sensation, swearing after *this*, the focus is all on her for the rest of the night.

I don’t last five minutes before I blow in her mouth. She hums, sucks, and licks me clean. When I finally open my eyes she’s sitting back on her heels with a little grin lighting up her face. I brush my hand over her cheek. “That was perfect.” I sit back on the bed and pat the spot next to me. “Now come up here so I can violate your ass.”

More eager than I would expect after that invitation, she’s up and over my lap. She shivers as I lean over and open my nightstand drawer. I drop a bottle of lube and the biggest anal plug she’s seen yet right in front of her face.

“That’s still not as big as your dick.”

Fuck, this woman kills me. “Thanks, baby girl.”

She grumbles and tucks her arms under her chest. All her soft skin, rubbing against me feels good. She’s right where she should be. Now that my dick’s calmed down, I’m able to think clearly. I start off slow, massaging and rubbing her down until she's limp. "Feel good?"

"Mmmmm-hmmm."

Perfect.

Slow and steady I make my way to her ass, dribbling lube down her crack and rubbing, stretching her wide. My finger teases her entrance and it's the first time she hasn't tensed up on me. Slowly, I push my finger in, the lube making it nice and easy. She groans in pleasure and shifts in my lap.

"Still good?"

"Yes," she whispers.

I spend some time working her open with my fingers before even bothering with the plug. This one's bigger than any of the others, but damn if I'm not finally fucking her ass tonight. Especially after she specifically and filthily asked me to. Reaching into the drawer again, I pull out a vibrator, she's only used it once—to put on a show for me—but when I hand it to her, she immediately knows what I want. She shifts and adjusts to get it where she wants before flicking it on.

"Oh my God."

Yeah, the vibrations are strong enough that I'm even getting stirred up again.

"Good girl. Keep it there. I want you to come while I'm playing with your ass."

"Oh. Oh." She moans and trembles.

"Jesus, already?"

She doesn't answer, so while she's still riding that out, I get to work slowly pushing the plug in, until the flat base is nestled between her cheeks. "Perfect."

Karina

"We're going to Luck's house. That okay with you, baby girl?"

It seems odd, but I'm curious about where Luck lives since I've only ever seen him at the clubhouse or our house. "Sure."

The ride there is...interesting with my ass full of Dante's giant toy. I swear he just loves tormenting me and never plans to actually fuck my ass.

Luck's house is a low, Spanish-style home with a solid wall around it, giving lots of privacy from his neighbors. I can only imagine why he needs that.

There's a strange pull in the air and I can't help wondering if I'm missing something as Luck meets us in the driveway and we follow him inside.

He offers us drinks and we stand around in the living room for few minutes. Much to my embarrassment, that strange sensation of being utterly alone with these two fierce, tempting men washes over me again. They could right now, right here in the middle of Luck's living room hold me down, strip off all my clothes and do whatever they wanted to me. I'd be powerless to do anything but scream, and cry and beg for mercy.

This time, the images in my head are much more vivid. Even though I've been trying to deny it for weeks, it's time I admit I'm a little attracted to Luck.

What's wrong with me? Dante should be more than enough for any woman.

It doesn't matter. I'd never act on those feelings.

I shift, rubbing my thighs together, desperately wishing Dante had let me wear panties.

As always, he's in tune with my moods. One corner of his mouth lifts in a sexy smirk. "You okay, baby girl?"

I can't get out a single word, so I nod. They exchange a look and Luck cocks his head to the side. "You want to see the rest of the house?"

By the rest of the house, Luck meant his bedroom. The three of us end up there. Dante closes the door behind us and my heart speeds up. Luck's watching me with an intent expression that brings heat to my skin.

Behind me, Dante settles his hands on my shoulders, pulling the straps of my tanktop down, exposing my bra. "Remember when we talked about stuff that turned you on?" He leans down closer, whispering in my ear. "How you said you wanted to try taking two cocks at once?"

"Did I?" I squeak out.

"Yes, you did."

Luck still hasn't said anything. But he's watching me like he wants to eat me alive. I'm scared and thrilled and so many other emotions, I can't speak.

"You know how you like it when I take my hand to your ass?"

I blush at him saying this in front of someone else, which is stupid. He's probably told Luck all sorts of things to prepare for tonight. In no way do I think we ended up here by accident.

"Luck's an expert on all sorts of other instruments to use on you."

I raise my eyes to Luck's face, seeking confirmation and he nods.

"Remember how you told me you wanted to be tied to the foot of the bed?"

I nod numbly. My skin's hot and tight all over. I'm so embarrassed he's revealing all my horny fantasies to someone else.

But I'm also crazily turned on.

Dante brushes the backs of his fingers over my cheek. "He's also good at all the different ways to tie naughty little girls up."

An ugly thought enters my mind that I can't shake. "Wait, have you guys...do you do this—"

"No, baby girl. We've never done this to anyone but you."

"Oh, good."

Luck chuckles at my jealous reaction.

Dante runs his hands over my body in a gesture meant to be soothing. Instead it works me up even more.

"Luck teaches classes on this stuff. Instead of learning by watching him do that to someone else, I thought he could demonstrate on you."

"Oh."

Dante chuckles. "You sound disappointed."

"No. I just thought you were going to..."

"If things are going well and you're still into it, we'll definitely fuck you, Karina," Luck says.

"Oh," I whisper and the guys chuckle.

Luck holds out his hand and after getting a nod from Dante, I take it. He stops next to the bed and settles his fingers under my chin. "Look at me. You want to stop at any time, or you're uncomfortable, say *red* and we'll know you're serious. Everything stops."

"Red. Okay."

He holds my chin a little firmer. "I'm serious. Don't think you're going to make me mad or that Dante will be mad at you. This is about you enjoying some new things, not enduring stuff to make us happy. Got it?"

Okay maybe it's a good thing I'm not wearing panties, they'd be soaked by now and I'd have to take them off anyway. "Got it."

Satisfied with my answer, he turns to Dante. "Can she finish undressing?"

Oh my God. Holy shit, am I really going to get naked in front of both of them?

Dante nods at me and I pull my tank top off the rest of the way. Next I work my shorts open and let them slide down my legs.

"No underwear. What a naughty girl," Luck teases.

"Turn around, Karina," Dante orders.

My face flames red as I turn and hear Luck inhale a sharp breath. "Very nice." His hand settles on my ass, wiggling the plug. A soft moan drifts from my lips and my legs tremble. Luck's arm bands around my waist, keeping me upright. His big, hard body connects with my back and I meet Dante's eyes. He's watching every move. Knowing he's right there and won't let anything bad happen, lessens the uneasy fluttering in my chest. Our eyes lock, intense even in the dim lighting.

Is he testing me?

Will he be mad if I enjoy this? *Should* I feel guilty about how much I'm enjoying Luck's hands roaming over my skin?

Dante finally moves in closer and I reach out. Our

fingers twine together and he steps close enough that his comforting heat washes over me.

Behind me, Luck closes his fist around my hair, brushing it over one shoulder. His lips press against my neck.

This can't be real. Both of these beyond-sexy bikers touching me, so completely focused on me at the same time. They're so similar, yet different. Dante—gruff, harsh, bulging with muscles. Luck—a more controlled roughness, leaner but just as hard.

"We should explain the ground rules to her," Luck says. His hot breath tickles my over-sensitive skin and I resist the urge to moan.

Dante lifts my chin and waits until I meet his eyes before speaking. "No kissing on the mouth. No fucking. Anything else is fair game."

"Nod if you understand, Karina," Luck says.

My eyes snap open, I hadn't even realized I'd closed them. Dante fills my vision. With his thick, dark hair, possessive stare and stubble-roughened chin, he's lethally sexy. My heart kicks up a notch. He's all mine. If this was *his* fantasy. If he wanted me and another girl there's no way I'd agree.

Or would I?

I think it's pretty obvious I'll do anything Dante asks.

I'm having trouble focusing with Luck's hard body behind me, his fingers curled over my shoulders. Not enough to hurt, but enough to feel his presence. Slowly, his hands slide down my arms, knuckles lightly grazing the sides of my bare breasts.

"She's fucking perfect, Dante."

Dante answers without taking his eyes off mine. "I know."

"Do you trust us, Karina?" Luck asks.

I don't have to even think about the answer. "Yes."

"Why?"

His follow-up question confuses me. *Why?* I don't know why. "Uh..." I stop and try to find the right words, but it's hard with Dante watching every reaction and Luck's rough hands stroking my skin. "Dante wouldn't let anything bad happen to me. And, uh, you've always been nice to me."

Behind me, Luck's chest vibrates with a humming sound of approval. "That's good," he says while placing a soft kiss on my cheek. His hands glide down my arms one last time and circle my wrists. He pauses and puts space between our bodies. Curious about what's next, I lower my gaze when he drops my left hand. As he grasps my right wrist in both of his big hands, I'm overcome with how fragile I am. *Red* was the magic word if I need to stop, but what if I said it and they just kept going?

I'm so wet from the thought, I press my thighs together. Dante notices and one corner of his mouth lifts, but he doesn't say anything.

Luck's arm drops to my waist, supporting me while he leans over. The sound of a drawer sliding open and shuffling makes me turn my head.

"Eyes on me, Karina," Dante says.

Heat races over my skin and my gaze snaps to him. He chuckles and I let out a sigh.

"For tonight, since it's her first time with anything like this, I'm going to show you something real basic," Luck says to Dante. There's a clink. "Safety shears. Always keep 'em handy."

Dante nods, watching everything Luck's doing behind me. Corded twine settles across my chest and Luck slowly massages it over my skin. "Preparing her for the rope," Luck explains. "Letting her get to know it."

Any other time, I think Dante might smirk, but instead, he crosses his arms over his chest and watches every move Luck makes.

The rope tickles but I'm too worked up to laugh. I let out a startled gasp as the twisted strands rub over my sensitized nipples. Finally, Luck brings the rope to my right hand.

"I'll start with a simple rope cuff." Luck lifts my arm in the air to demonstrate. "I'm using a ten foot piece of six millimeter hemp rope, but you can experiment and see what you like."

Dante asks a few questions while Luck wraps the rope around my wrist, but I'm too hypnotized to really pay attention.

"The wider you make the band, the more comfortable it will be for her." Luck's voice breaks through my fog and I notice he's got both wrists bound. "Especially if you want to string her up for long periods of time and really work her over."

Luck slides his hand up my body, between my breasts and lightly curls his hand over my throat. "Is that what you told Dante you wanted?" he asks against my ear. His voice is low enough to make my tummy flutter, but loud enough for Dante to hear every word.

It takes me a couple seconds to form a response. "Yes," I whisper.

"Can you tell me why?"

No. I can't explain it. I swallow hard, feeling Luck's fingers around my neck with each movement before answering. "I don't know. I like...I like the feeling...it feels safe," I murmur.

A low, sexy growl vibrates against my ear and Luck cups my breasts, gently stroking and teasing my already hard nipples. My brain slips a little more into a soft fuzziness.

"I can show you how to bind her breasts, too. She'd look nice all roped up."

"Can we suspend her from something? Tie her legs wide open?" Dante asks. I can't tell if he's serious or teasing. Not that it matters, if he wants me strung-up and spread-eagle, I'll happily do it.

Luck laughs softly. "Sure. I don't have suspension equipment here, but the place I told you about does."

"Nice." Dante moves closer. Heat radiates from his body, sinking into mine. The back of his hand rubs over my cheek and I lean into his touch. "You're so beautiful."

My tongue's too fuzzy to answer with words. "Mmm..."

"She goes under easy," Luck says to Dante.

Dante tilts his head to the side, inviting Luck to explain. "Subspace..."

I don't need to hear the explanation. He's right. I'm completely gone as soon as Dante comes near me. Having him hand me over to someone else just as capable while he stands and watches with heat in his eyes has pretty much turned me into fluffy jelly.

I giggle at the idea of jelly being fluffy.

Both of them stop talking. "You okay, baby girl?" Dante asks.

"Mmm..." A warm tingly sensation spreads from my scalp to the tips of my ears.

Luck pulls me back against him, a little harder this time. His erection digs into my back, hard and demanding. Hard enough to snap my eyes open.

I like Luck. I'm definitely attracted to him. This whole scene has me turned on like crazy. But something feels so wrong for a reason I can't pinpoint. And not the *good* kind of wrong I usually feel when Dante does dirty things to me. My heart flutters, but I can't force my mouth to form any words.

Dante cups my chin, demanding without words that I meet his eyes. Clearly he reads the panic in mine.

"Do you want to stop, Karina?"

"She might not be able to answer," Luck says. He's right. My tongue still feels like cotton balls.

Dante fingers the ropes still binding my wrists. "Maybe this is good for our first lesson."

CHAPTER FOURTEEN

DANTE

Karina's quiet the whole way home. I'm worried I might've pushed her too far. Admitting she's turned on by the thought of two guys going at her and then actually *doing* it are two different things. Especially for someone her age.

I'm a stubborn fuck, so I don't want to admit that while it was real fuckin' hot watching Luck bind her wrists and get her worked up, the idea of her getting on her knees for anyone but me made me want to pull out my nine millimeter and blow a hole through my brother's chest.

As soon as we're in our room, she starts sobbing.

"I'm sorry I ruined everything."

Not what I wanted at all from tonight. "Shh. Nothing to be sorry about. I told you if you weren't into it, we weren't gonna do it." I wrap her up in my arms and she sags against me.

"Luck probably hates me."

All Luck had been concerned about was me taking her home and caring for her. "No, baby girl. He's fine."

"I didn't want you to be mad at me later or—"

I press my palms to the sides of her face. "Hey. Told you, baby. The only thing that would ever make me mad at you is you lyin' to me. As long as you always tell me the truth, we're good."

"Okay."

My hand drifts lower, finding her tiny shorts soaked. "Tonight excited you a little." I don't bother phrasing it as a question.

"Yes," she moans as I rub her pussy harder through the material. I wrap her hair around my fist and tug her head back so I can mash my lips against hers. "You still my horny little slut?"

"Fuck, yes." Her words come out soft and breathless.

"Frustrated?"

"Yes," she whines.

"You need to come, don't you?"

"Please?"

I rip her shorts off so fast, the button goes flying across the room. "On the bed."

She's so needy and frustrated she doesn't even try to tease me. She lies back exactly the way I've taught her. My face is in her cunt, tongue lapping at her, lips sucking at her clit and minutes later she's coming. When she stops yelling, I flip her over, yank the plug out and replace it with my cock. The lube's still sitting on the bed from earlier and I reach over to grab it, coating my dick with a nice layer as I fight my way inside her tight little ass. She yelps, but pushes back against me instead of trying to get away. I slide into her for what feels like forever. She wriggles and that last little push is exactly what I needed to get all the way in. My balls rest against her pussy and she's pulsing around my cock so hard, I stop to catch my breath.

Fuck, her ass is fucking tighter than hell.

She turns her head so I can see her face, her eyes. The sassy little bitch raises an eyebrow at me.

"You're looking for it, baby girl."

She laughs and fists her hands in the bedspread, but keeps her eyes on me.

I pull out and slide right back in. Her eyelids flutter shut and she moans.

"Yeah, baby girl likes my dick in her ass, doesn't she?"

"You're filthy."

"Fuck, yeah I am. You're a pretty filthy girl, too."

"Only with you. Only *for* you."

Fuck. She has my balls and my heart in the palm of her hand. "You're really beautiful right now, Karina."

"Thank you, daddy."

"Your tiny little asshole looks perfect stretched around my dick.

She clenches again and I take in a shaky breath.

"I feel...I need..."

"Touch yourself. Play with your clit while I pound your ass."

She gets to work rubbing herself, trembling and shaking under me. I slide in farther and lean over her, keeping my weight on my arms. "Good?"

"Yes," she moans. "Is it bad that it feels this good?"

"No, baby."

"Harder."

She doesn't have to say that twice. I slide in and out a little faster, still being careful. Fuck this feels good, and I'm so fuckin' happy she seems to like it, because we need to do this again and again.

"Dante. So close."

"Let go." I'm telling her to let go, but I'm the one who lets loose pounding into her while she shudders and sobs under me.

I yank her hair back so I can see her face and the little smile she gives me sends me right over the edge. I pull out and unload all over her back and ass while she sighs into the mattress. There's lube and cum everywhere, but I give her a second to come down before throwing her into the shower.

"We need to try that again," she says as I soap her down.

"Liked it, huh?"

"Is that bad?"

"Not to me."

"Can we do it other ways?" she asks with an excited edge. "So I can see you better."

"We can do it any way you want. Bend over." I inspect her ass for any damage and hell, because I enjoy looking at her ass. "You feel okay?"

"I'm a little sore. But a good sore."

"All right. I'll leave your ass alone for now. Tell me how you feel in the morning. I went at you pretty hard at the end there."

She shivers. "I know."

CHAPTER FIFTEEN

DANTE

"I CAN'T BELIEVE you're letting her come with us," Karina whispers as we head downstairs the evening after I violated the hell out of her ass.

"She's been bugging you about it for months. It's her birthday, she can come."

Between Athena nagging my girl and Romeo nagging *me*, I'm ready to just let them at each other and fuck the consequences. Ain't my fucking concern.

"I'm more pissed we can't take my bike," I say as I turn and press her up against the wall. Tonight I'm gonna explain the club's claiming ritual to her. The pull I feel toward Karina, the love I have for her's stronger than fuckin' ever. Making her mine permanently feels right. Maybe not tonight or tomorrow, but I want her getting used to the idea.

I grind my hips into her so she can feel exactly how much I don't want to leave our bedroom and head to the clubhouse tonight. We spent the day apart. Me at the clubhouse patching in Cricket and his buddy. Her, celebrating Athena's birthday all day. I thought we'd have the night alone. But Athena followed her home and asked about the party being held at the clubhouse.

"I'll drive my own car," Athena volunteers from the living room.

"What is she, part bat?" I ask Karina, who giggles and pulls away from me. Her ass twitches as she hops down the stairs, reminding me of the plug I just shoved in her. At *her* request. I've created an anal-loving little monster.

I can't wait to get her alone in our room at the clubhouse.

ROMEO ZEROES in on me as soon as I walk in the door. His gaze skips to Karina and I swear I see a hint of disappointment. Then Athena stumbles in behind me and his face goes positively wolfish at the sight of her. He smooths the eager look away and saunters over.

"What's up, brother?" His tone almost conveys casual.

Karina presses up against my side. Romeo still freaks her out, which doesn't bother me a bit. After that clusterfuck last night, my inclination was to lock her up in my bedroom. "Hi, Romeo," she says shyly. "Athena and I spent the day with her family for her *birthday* and she asked if it would be okay if she came to the party tonight. I hope that's okay?" I cough to cover up my laughter at the way she stresses birthday. Just in case Romeo forgot Athena's finally legal.

Like the prick he is, Romeo's mouth curves into a

wicked smile. "That right?" He lifts his chin at Athena. "Is today your birthday, sweetheart?" he asks her.

For all her chatter this evening Athena turns pink and shies away once Romeo focuses his attention on her. "Yes."

God help me.

I heave out a deep breath and pull Romeo aside. Karina leads Athena over to the bar, giving us some privacy.

"Listen, I ain't got no say over what you do with your dick, brother. But I feel responsible for her, being she's Karina's friend and all. Treat her with care, please."

For once he drops his smirk and takes my warning seriously. "Yeah. She'll be okay with me. I won't let her out of my sight."

He seems sincere, so I walk over to the bar to collect my girl.

"Athena." Her head snaps up at the sound of my voice, and her eyes widen when she spots Romeo behind me. "We'll be upstairs. You need anything, call your girl," I say with a nod at Karina.

"Okay."

I've waited long enough. My hand captures Karina's and I practically drag her upstairs. She stumbles and runs to catch up with me.

"Dante, should we really leave her alone down there?"

"She'll be fine." I work the lock on our door open and shove her inside. "Romeo's a dick, but he won't let anything bad happen to her."

Her nose scrunches up in a way that says she's not so sure, but she doesn't want to disagree with me. "Okay."

"Now, no more talking about them. I want to focus on us."

She gives me a slight smile. "I like the sound of that." She wriggles against the door, clearly uncomfortable.

"How's that ass?"

"Full," she answers with a pissy-pouty face that's cute as fuck. *No.* Can't get distracted. I take both her hands in mine and lead her to the bed. "I need to talk to you."

Karina

THE SUDDEN SERIOUS turn in our fun conversation unnerves me. I haven't forgotten the way we left Luck's last night. Dante said he wasn't mad, but I'm still unsure.

The explosive, fire-cracking sex certainly helped.

I shift, a little uncomfortable, but like the small reminder of last night's activities.

Dante rubs my hands between us. He seems almost nervous. I've never seen him anything but confident or lethal.

"You remember when people have said you're going to be my ol' lady?"

"Yes. Sadie said it's a really special thing to you guys and not every woman gets to be one."

"That's right. It means my brothers trust you and will protect you with their last breath."

"Does it make me your wife?"

"Sort of. In the eyes of the club, yeah, but it's more than that."

"Oh." Why is he telling me this?

"We do things a little differently in this club. Not totally unheard of, but a bit extreme."

"Oh, God. You're not going to brand me with a hot poker or something, are you?"

He laughs so hard the bed shakes and I smack his arm. "Stop laughing at me."

His hands frame my face and he pulls me forward for a rough kiss. "I fuckin' love the crazy shit that comes out of your mouth sometimes."

"Well, you said *extreme*."

"Then it's going to seem tame to you after that."

"Can't I just get your name tattooed on me or something?"

He gaze roams over me so slow my skin burns.

"Yeah. I want you to get *Dante's Baby Girl*, right here," he says, grazing his fingers over my hip area. "But that can wait until you're a little older."

I'm not complaining. Needles freak me out. I *am* impatient though. "So what is *it?*"

"You know how you're not allowed in the chapel?"

"Yes," I groan.

"Well for this you will be. To claim you in the eyes of my brothers, I need to fuck you on our table in front of the entire club."

My jaw drops and I just stare at him for a minute, absorbing that scenario.

"Do they join in?" I finally ask.

"No. Fuck no. That's the whole point. They're watching me claim you as mine and no one else's."

"Prospects too?"

"Hell fucking no."

Okay, now that I think about it, the whole thing sounds kind of hot. I sort of like the idea of the guys standing there watching Dante take something they can never have.

"Do I have to be naked?"

"Fuck no."

"Okay."

He raises an eyebrow. "Okay?"

"I trust you."

A satisfied smile spreads across his face. "Thank you, baby girl."

"Wait a second. Are there any other surprises the Iron Bulls have in store for an ol'-lady-to-be that I should know about?"

Dante chuckles. "None that I can think of right now."

CHAPTER SIXTEEN

DANTE

KARINA TOOK THE WHOLE "CLAIMING" conversation a lot better than I expected. I'm still not sure it's going down right away, but at least I feel better about moving forward and having her around the club more.

The next morning we get the shock of finding Athena in Romeo's lap downstairs. I need way more coffee in my system before I deal with *that* situation. If Karina's surprised, she hides it well. She follows Athena into the kitchen and I can only imagine how that conversation will go.

When I turn, I find Romeo staring at the doors the girls just disappeared behind.

"So, was it everything you'd hoped?" I ask and barely manage to keep a straight face.

Romeo's eyes widen. He's *unsettled* and I'm dying to give him shit. He's certainly earned it after all the fucked-up jokes he's made about me and my girl.

"Tucker's on his way in," he informs me, ruining my plans for payback.

"What the fuck for?" The thought of seeing that slimy prick again ruins my good mood.

"He's got Kadence's info for you."

"Doesn't that asshole know how to pick up a phone or send a fucking text? Jesus Christ."

He lifts his chin and I see the girls have returned from the kitchen with coffee. They glance our way before settling down at the bar.

Romeo nods at Karina. "Just thought I'd warn you in case you wanted your woman to throw on more clothes."

I glance at my beautiful girl, wearing socks and one of my T-shirts that hangs to her knees and nothing else. She's perfect.

"Nah. Don't give two fucks what he thinks about us." I don't take my eyes off her and she must feel the weight of my stare, because she turns and gives me a soft, sweet smile.

I don't want anything wiping that smile off her face. As Romeo leaves to join the girls, I stop him with a hand on his arm. "Keep an eye on Karina. I'm going to meet him outside. Don't want him upsetting her today."

"Yeah, okay."

"Hey, I might be claiming her ass sooner than later."

"Yeah? How was that conversation?" It's hard to tell if he's fucking with me or he genuinely wants to know.

"None of your fucking business."

He glances over at Athena again.

"Aw, should we make it a double ceremony, prez?"

I get a sharp glare in return. "Fuck off."

After a brief discussion with Karina, I head outside to wait for Tucker. He rolls up maybe fifteen minutes later.

And he ain't exactly thrilled to find me waiting outside for him.

CHAPTER SEVENTEEN

KARINA

"I CAN *NOT* BELIEVE you're still here."

Athena isn't impressed with my harsh whisper. Her mouth curls into a sly smile, but I don't get to question her further.

Dante's big hands curl over my shoulder and his lips brush against my ear. "Baby girl, I need to take care of some business outside. You'll be okay for a few minutes?"

"Sure."

I notice Romeo's joined us and I'm not sure how I feel about that. It's a little too weird to think of my best friend and Romeo...*ew*.

All my concerns about whatever the heck they're doing are wiped away when I spot Luck entering the common area. "Be right back."

Athena's so wrapped up in Romeo, she doesn't even notice my departure.

"Luck?"

He stops and gives me a genuine smile. A flash from last night stops me.

Luck's hands on my breasts.

Skillfully tying my wrists.

His rich warm voice reverberating against my ear.

Heat sears my cheeks at the memories. Will I ever be able to look at him again without blushing?

"Karina? You okay?" he asks, coming closer.

I suck in a deep breath and lift my chin. "Can we talk?"

He stares at me for a second, then glances around the room. "Where's Dante?"

"Outside."

Gently, he places his hand on my shoulder and guides me into the hallway. "What is it, sweetheart?"

He's being so nice and it only makes me feel worse about the way things ended last night. "I'm sorry," I blurt out.

I risk a glance up into his eyes and only find concern. "There's nothing to be sorry about. I told you we wouldn't do anything you weren't comfortable with."

"I was. I wanted you... to do...but I just—"

Heat flares in his eyes and it stops any more babble from tumbling out of my mouth. "Did you like it?"

"What?"

"The ropes."

"Oh, yes. I think so. It's neat. The suspension stuff sounded cool."

For a brief moment he rubs the back of his hand over my cheek. "You're special, Karina. I hope Dante always treats you well."

I'm not sure if it's a question, concern, or statement, so I simply answer, "He does."

"Whenever you're ready, you guys can come over for another lesson. I'll leave it up to him."

"Okay."

I watch as he walks away, feeling like we had two very different conversations.

CHAPTER EIGHTEEN

DANTE

TUCKER MUST HAVE REACHED DOWN and found his balls since the last time I saw him. He scowls as if he remembers we're practically family and he ain't too fond of the idea.

Tough shit.

He flicks a piece of paper at me. "I got Kadence's number."

"And?" His blank face begs me to smash my fist into it. "You have that talk with her?"

Ballsy motherfucker grits his teeth before answering me. "Yes. It was very unpleasant."

"Life's gonna get a whole lot more *unpleasant* if you don't stop making me ask you questions. Tell me what the fuck I want to know so you can leave."

He finally drops the attitude. "At first she was pissed and hung up on me. But she called back and she's excited to meet Karina."

"Good."

"She's in California right now and won't be back until

next week though. Broke up with her boyfriend or something. I'm warning you, there's always some drama—"

A quick shake of my head shuts him up. "Ain't your concern. *I'll* take care of Karina."

By the look on his face he's annoyed he has no say over his younger daughter's life.

Too bad. He gave up that right a long time ago far as I'm concerned.

"You know her momma was involved with the Savage Dragons' prez, right?" he asks.

Like I give a fuck. "Don't concern me."

We stare at each other for a minute. He breaks eye contact first and finally hands over the information. "I'll give Karina the number and let her work things out with her *sister*."

The coward flinches, but doesn't contradict me. No, instead he follows me inside. Brave fucker.

Romeo must have warned Karina because she's nowhere to be found. Sadie stops me from tearing the place apart.

"She's upstairs."

"Thanks, Sadie-girl."

Karina smiles when I open the door to our room. She's perched on the bed reading a book, and looks so frickin' cute, I forget all about how much I wanted to beat the shit out of her dad five seconds ago.

"Got something for you, baby girl."

She closes the book and sits up. "What?"

Can't say I blame her for being a little wary. I've thrown a couple surprises at her in the last few days.

I drop down next to her on the bed. "Now, I don't

want you to get too excited. Nothing can happen until next week."

"You're killing me." She glances at the paper in my hand and bites her lip. "What is it?"

My other hand closes over hers. "Whatever happens, I'm here. You and me. What we have, no one can touch."

"Thank you." She meets my eyes and whispers. "You know I feel the same way, right?"

I can't help it. My hand cups the back of her head and I pull her to me for one of the softest kisses I've probably ever given her. "Yeah, baby girl. I know," I say against her lips. I brush one last kiss on her forehead and sit back.

Tucker's warning about Kadence's wildness and her mother's involvement with a rival MC is strong in my mind. I'll need to make sure the sisters have their first few meetings on *my* turf so I can keep Karina safe.

None of that's stuff she needs to worry about right now. I hand over the slip of paper and she unfolds it, reads it, then stares up at me with shining eyes.

"Ready to meet your sister, baby girl?"

ALSO BY PHOENYX SLAUGHTER

ASUNDER (Iron Bulls MC #1)
DISCONNECT (Iron Bulls MC #2)
ENTWINED (Iron Bulls MC #3)
VEXED (Iron Bulls MC #4)
UNHINGED (Iron Bulls MC #5)

DIRTY SIDE DOWN (Iron Bulls MC Boxed Set)
Includes Asunder, Disconnect, Entwined,
plus never-before released Bonus Scene.

Standalone novella
INFATUATION (A Rebel Stepbrother Romance)
Only available on select platforms.

IRON BULLS MC
PHOENYX SLAUGHTER

www.ingramcontent.com/pod-product-compliance
Lightning Source LLC
Chambersburg PA
CBHW061239170626
46809CB00007B/2741

* 9 7 8 1 9 4 3 9 5 0 8 3 6 *